THE HOUSE OF JASMINE

THE HOUSE OF JASMINE

by Ibrahim Abdel Meguid

Translated and with an afterword by Noha Radwan

Interlink Books

An imprint of Interlink Publishing Group, Inc.
Northampton, Massachusetts

Library of Congress Cataloging-in-Publication Data
'Abd al-Majid, Ibrahim.
[Bayt al-yasamin. English]
The house of jasmine / by Ibrahim Abdel Meguid; translated by Noha Radwan.
—1st American ed.
    p. cm.
 ISBN 978-1-56656-882-1 (pbk.)
1. Egypt—History—1970–1981—Fiction. I. Radwan, Noha M. II. Title.
PJ7804.M323B3913 2012
892.7'36—dc23
                    2011049566

Printed and bound in the United States of America
10 9 8 7 6 5 4 3 2 1

To request a copy of our 48-page full-color catalog, please call 1-800-238-LINK, visit our website at www.interlinkbooks.com, or write to:
Interlink Publishing, 46 Crosby Street, Northampton, MA 01060
info@interlinkbooks.com

I

The people hauled a corpse in a sack out of Mahmudiyya Canal and no sooner had they opened the sack, than they saw an amazingly beautiful woman slowly coming back to life. Horrified, they stepped away from her, and she turned into a column of fire. They were shocked, and dropped unconscious or dead, while she began running naked in the streets, her blond hair flying behind her, and everyone who looked at her was charmed, began running after her, and was lost without a trace. . .

I had not thought about this ahead of time or planned for it. I had been wondering, ever since the bus filled up with the sixty workers and left the shipyard gate, why they had chosen me. There was no reason for me to be afraid, but at the same time I didn't feel particularly encouraged.

The bus went down Maks Street, through Qabbari, then Kafr 'Ashri and Basal Port, and entered Saba' Banat Street, and all the while I neither spoke to anybody nor did anybody speak to me.

How did I fail to note the journey? It's only a short distance, but it's quite distinctive, for at the intersection at the end of Maks Street there is always a traffic jam, the intersection is always crowded with carts, trucks, trailers, the bus and the tram, and you can always hear a woman shouting. Suddenly the tranquility of the rest of Maks Street and the serenity of the buildings on both sides of it disappear. This serenity always makes you feel that you are walking alone and at night, but after that damned intersection, the noise never ceases to plague you. As soon as you reach al-Tarikh Bridge, the smell of stored cotton and jute assails you—a musty smell mixed with that of the grains stored in the ancient granaries of the credit bank. You see a man urinating against the wall of the granaries and another defecating by the wall with his face to the street. The road becomes rough, and the bus goes bumping over it, while the tram, which is usually running alongside the bus, rattles on. When you reach the intersection of Basal Port, where Khedive and Saba' Banat streets meet, the air becomes refreshingly cooler, because of the height of the buildings and the width of Khedive Street, which ends at the port. There you can sleep in peace. But we have passed all this. . .

My head almost hit the roof when I stood up. I bent a little and surveyed their faces. I felt like shouting insults at them for their eerie silence. I smiled. Alexandria is usually filled with bright light at this time of the year, her sea stretching leisurely into the distance, while the windows of her houses open like a woman drying her hair in the sunlight, and the girls stroll cheerfully in the streets.

I knew that the sudden traffic jam from Sidi Gabir Station to the white palace of Ras al-Tin would not disturb the city, would not mar her appearance. And here she was: indifferent to it all. Now I was out of that traffic jam, but Saba' Banat Street seemed to be at peace with the vehicles driving on it, with the stores on its sides open but quiet. Later I heard one of the people who had been in the traffic jam say that it didn't last long, and I can testify to that account, for how could you otherwise explain the relaxed atmosphere of Saba' Banat Street, as if what happened in the city didn't concern it?

This little city is enchanted; she can rid herself of her garbage even when the garbage collectors and street sweepers don't appear on her streets. It's as if she had an agreement with secret ghosts to keep her beautiful.

"Of course you know that you will each get half a pound after the reception. . ." I said.

". . ."

"What do you say you each take a quarter of a pound now, and then just leave?" I said, and I must have frowned, because I felt my eyes getting wider.

"You mean we don't get to see Nixon?" one of them asked.

"It's up to you if you see him or not," another answered.

The driver stopped the bus when I told him to, and the workers got off, laughing. I don't think that the traffic policeman at the end of the street cared about the bus blocking the intersection of Haqqaniyya marketplace, obstructing the tram and the pedestrian crossing.

As for my mother, who must have been in the small courtyard of the house, throwing wet bread crumbs to the chickens, I don't think that her heart fluttered, or her chest felt tight, at the moment when her son, who had the strange name, committed a crime. . .

❀

It was not yet past one o'clock when I found myself on the sidewalk in front of Crystal Café, where I had been sitting to watch. The motorcade had passed, and the crowds had slipped down the side alleys leading to Manshiyya and Raml Station. The space around me appeared white and clear, with the endless blue sea, the immense sky, and me standing alone as if I had showed up after the end of the world. I almost laughed at the thought of a new world beginning with me. Then I shivered. It would be difficult to be Adam, and more difficult to have a world empty of everybody except me.

I hadn't noticed that the people who had lined the sidewalk along the seashore had crossed the street. Maybe they all retreated and fell into the sea. I saw a single man in the distance, where the shore curves and disappears and the pier to the castle of Qaitbay seems to extend from the tall buildings that occupy the view. Maybe the people followed the motorcade to the palace, and this man was their tail end. But enough time hasn't passed for that. And I wouldn't have missed it.

I pictured the president's wide, radiant smile, and Nixon's astonished smile, his red face and prominent cheeks, his right arm waving as if painting an endless wall. On both sides of the convertible, which was as wide as some mythical duck, there were two Americans, whose eyes were fixed on the high windows overlooking the street. Each had his hand resting on a gun at his side. Why was the one on the water's edge looking up, when there was nothing over the sea but the open sky?

I stuck my hands in my pockets, spat the cigarette butt out of my mouth in the skillful manner that I had now mastered, and walked on, thinking about my mind and the strange ways in which it was working.

Sixty times a quarter of a pound equals fifteen. I made twelve. I thought of giving the driver five pounds, because I figured that any money that he got would implacate him in the act, but then I gave him three, and smiled at the slyness with which I was suddenly acting.

I crossed Chamber of Commerce Street, and entered Sa'ad Zaghlul Street. I glanced to my left and saw people sitting outside the Brazilian coffee store drinking coffee. The girls' skirts were so tight that they revealed the elastic of their panties digging into their firm flesh, and their bras showed through their light shirts.

"Cappuccino," I said to the man behind the espresso machine, who then looked up at me. Is there anything wrong? Is it because I am tall? Because I have come into the store alone? There were young couples sitting and whispering in every corner of the store. Standing alone among them, I discovered that I could not look around. It would be an invasion of their privacy, and would oblige people to raise their eyes quite high to look back at me.

"Pardon!" said a girl who almost bumped into me as she hurried into the store. Then she took a step backward, and nearly fell down the steps at the entrance. I held her arm, and felt my fingers press into her soft flesh. The smell of her perfume invaded and shattered me. It seemed as if my clothes fluttered and my nose widened at the invasion. I bought a news-paper from a nearby newsstand, and walked away with the sensation of her cool skin still on my fingers. I didn't care what the man behind the espresso machine said when I left before he had finished fixing my coffee.

On Safiyya Zaghlul Street, I realized that my feet alone were deciding my route. I love this street, and no one has ever liked the Alhambra Cinema as much as I used to. It used to open early in the day, so students always slipped in. It's probably the same now. We used to wait for a full hour before the movie started. The washed floors had a familiar smell, the faint lamps were spread far apart on both sides of the theater, and there was the distinct light of the bathroom. There was a spontaneous seating arrangement, as if whole schools had come into the theater and not just individual students. And there were the exchanges of insults:

"The School of Commerce at Muharram Bey salutes the Crafts School. May God provide! May God provide! Seven crafts in hand, but it's luck we demand. Tra la la la." "Alexandria School of Crafts salutes Abbasiah High. Rain falls from the sky, out of water fish die!" "Abbasiah High salutes the School of Commerce. Spiro Spatis betrayed the nation. Spiro Spatis betrayed the nation. . . " Meanwhile, the light of the bathroom remained distinctly visible.

It was quite a while before the show started. Then came the famous song: "My beloved nation, my grand nation, day after day its glories increase and its life fills with victories. My nation is growing and becoming liberated. My nation. My nation." Everyone sang along. Then came the cheer: "Long live the good-for-nothing generation!"

As the movie started, so did the whistling, while the light of the bathroom remained distinctively visible. The steam engine runs between Marilyn Monroe's thighs, Jack Lemmon lets his boss use his apartment so that he can bring Shirley

6

MacLaine to it. Raf Vallone rapes Sophia Loren at the coal store. Gina Lollobrigida jumps into the circus ring with Tony Curtis. Burt Lancaster smiles idiotically at Gary Cooper. Kirk Douglas sadly touches the belly of Jean Simmons, who is pregnant with his son, the son of Spartacus. Jacques Sernas kidnaps Rossana Podesta, and starts the Trojan War. Steve Reeves plucks out a tree and throws it in front of the cart whose horses have bolted. A strange man sitting next to me says that he knew this Hercules personally before he got into the movies. The door to the bathroom opens every minute, and while my face remains turned towards the screen, my animal calls for that door. When I feel its heat on my thighs, I spread my legs a little, and then I get up. I am not the only one spilling himself on the bathroom floor. It's very crowded, and each person is looking intently at the floor to hide the well-known secret. All I see are bushy heads of hair. . . .

Why do I remember all these useless details now? It's all over, and it wasn't even a conscious decision on my part. I don't go to the movies or think about my animal anymore. Is it possible that I have forgotten about it? Well, it shouldn't distract me now. I should only look ahead.

The street was as clean as it always is. It gave me the familiar feeling that it was mine, that I was the one who designed it and designated its beginning and end. Here was the usual morning breeze blowing gently with the taste of fresh spring water. The noon sun shed only its brightest and most tender rays. It seemed as if it had been years since I last walked down this street. Why am I suddenly realizing all of this?

I thought of throwing the newspaper in the nearest trash can so I could be alone. I was busy catching the breeze, which was scented with women's perfumes. My eyes raced with the

7

sun's rays over their brilliant legs. I didn't want to sit in the spacious and loud billiard hall. Hani always won there. I had run into him three years ago near the telephone office. He was laughing constantly, as he usually was. How can a sergeant in the army laugh so hard in a public square? But I was glad. He didn't ignore me. I asked him if Rashid still knew all of 'Abd al-Halim's songs by heart. He said that Rashid had finished medical school, and joined the army, and that he didn't see him anymore. The army is a big place. . . He also said that no one left the army these days.

"Haven't you been drafted by the army?" he asked.

"I am an only son, as you know," I answered.

"So you are responsible for the home front," he said, and giggled freely. Then he told me that it had been a long time since he came to this place at Raml Station, and that he was there to call his fiancée in Cairo. Then he left.

❀

"Breaded scallopini," I said.

"I'm sorry, but we don't have that today," said the handsome black waiter. I didn't know what else to order, and I hadn't realized there was a menu on the table. At Elite, there are always couples on dates, and you can always hear them kissing. Hani used to tell us amazing stories. He said that he joined the military academy to get the most girls to fall in love with him. What brought me to Elite just now?

I had stopped in front of Rialto Cinema, enchanted by the pictures hanging outside the box office. The Jane Mansfield picture was still at the center, her big bosom almost ready to jump into my hands. But I have stopped collecting her

8

postcard photographs to take into the bathroom with me at home. I have stopped buying postcard photographs altogether, and the factories have also stopped producing bars of soap with pictures of nude women on their wrappers. It must have been a government decision. It must also have been the government who changed the kinds and brands of soap. It didn't know that I had already, without any conscious decision, quit my bad habit.

I hadn't thrown away the newspaper yet. I let it fall out of my hand. Then I saw a young couple looking at the pictures while holding hands. They were glancing at me, then whispering to each other and smiling. I bent down to pick up the newspaper, and felt a pain in my stomach, so I crossed the street and went into Elite.

"Why is there no scallopini?"

"There are no eggs. We ran out unexpectedly."

"Shrimp then. Large grilled shrimp, and beer."

I wasn't going to retreat. At the tables, young men sat with women ripe with both femininity and happiness, and the music was what you could call dreamy. Why this silence following my entry? The atmosphere may be sweet but it also invites sleep. With no kisses or whispers around me, I lit a cigarette, found the menu on the table, and started reading it. Will there be more orders to take the workers out to greet the President? He always visits Alexandria on the twenty-sixth of July. He practically moves his headquarters to Alexandria during the summer now. My fortune, therefore, lies with those who will visit the President during the summer. But. . . Oh God! The relationship between Egypt and Syria has been strained, between Egypt and Libya, between Egypt and the Soviet Union, between Egypt and the Palestinians. That's four

9

leaders who will not visit Egypt this year, and perhaps even more.

The waiter placed a bottle of beer on my table, and I drank it all. My stomach hurt. I drank the beer like water on an empty stomach. Then came the shrimp, their powerful aroma preceding them as the waiter hurried to the table. I thought that I should put some food in my stomach quickly. I ordered a second beer. My only hope is the twenty-sixth of July. What if he actually moves his headquarters to Alexandria before then? There won't be any receptions. He cannot visit Alexandria if he is already here. Then it is all a matter of luck. I had a headache, which was strongest at the front of my head. I had never had beer before.

I left after paying a whole six pounds, half the revenue of Nixon's visit. There were rumors in the city about American ships unloading mounds of butter and powdered milk, rumors so strong that Hassanayn told me yesterday that the people of the Bahari and Anfushi neighborhoods were hogging the foodstuffs and keeping them from everyone else. It was also said that American marines were giving out dollars in Manshiyya, that helicopters were dropping sacks of flour tied to parachutes of Japanese silk, and that the parachutes were even better than the flour, because the cloth was so soft that it was perfect for making lingerie... None of this was true. The only person who gained anything from Nixon's visit was me, at least so far. It's a shame that Alexandria didn't know that, and that I had wasted half of what I made. I was afraid that I might collapse on the street with my headache, drunkenness, and stuffed stomach. It would be loud and comical, like the collapse of the Hafi Building. A tall person should never get drunk. Why did I take this little tour? Is this what thieves do?

I had planned to buy a new dress and a pair of shoes for my mother. Why did I forget?

❀

It was past three o'clock when I stood in front of the entrance of Elite. I was covered with sweat and the weather was scorching. The noise and glitter of Safiyya Zaghlul Street disappointed me.

"Can you take me to Dikhayla?"

"Of course," answered the cab driver with a smirk. I wasn't sure whether he was smirking at my height, at my posture as I bent down, or at the smell of beer coming from my mouth, but I couldn't care less about such happy people. I fell asleep, and he woke me up after we had passed Maks. I wiped away the sweat flowing down my neck. I gave him a whole pound, twice what he deserved, and he was grateful.

The first thing that struck me about my house was its untiled floor. My father had covered the floor with an uneven layer of concrete seven years ago. I took off my clothes and hung them on a hanger next to all my other clothes. I put on my pajamas and found a five-piaster coin in one of the pockets. When and why did I put it there? Mother was taking a nap, so she must have eaten lunch alone and not waited for me. I lay down in bed and lit a cigarette. I tried to blow the smoke strongly to make it reach the wooden ceiling, but it didn't. I must have left the newspaper at Elite. I thought of selling the house, and of following international politics in the news-papers. What is this sudden sexual appetite?

❀

I saw my mother standing wearily at the door staring at me, as if in disbelief that I had come home alone. If only the President would visit Alexandria on Mother's Day!

"What's the matter with you, Shagara?"[1]

"Nothing. Just thinking about getting married."

[1] Shagara, the narrator's name, means "tree."

2

*After the 1967 defeat, there appeared a man with bare feet,
ragged clothes, and a thick beard and mustache, who roamed the
streets of Qabbari. He often stopped to yell: "Fuck the Empire
where the sun never sets!" And he would beat a dog he kept and
called Johnson. A year later another dog appeared with him,
which he called Jacqueline, and a third, which he called U Thant.
Then there were more dogs, whom he called Brent, Mobutu,
Indira, Lord Caradon, Golda, Elizabeth, Pompidou, and so on.
This parade became quite a sight, and people always opened their
windows to watch it. The children ran after him yelling: "Fuck
the Empire where the sun never sets!"*

*There were, however, two unforgettable days. The first was
the day his dog Johnson died, and he got drunk and lay down
on the sidewalk crying bitterly, the dog's body on his lap. The
other dogs, which he had also gotten drunk, were swaying from
side to side, and barking sadly, interrupted by hiccups, which no
one had thought dogs could get. And then there was the day last
week when the man himself died, and his dogs roamed the streets
alone yelling: "Fuck the Empire where the sun never sets!"*

The next day was the coldest and most depressing day of my life. Every minute, I thought that someone must have reported what I had done, and that the word had spread as quickly as the shipyard's machinery turned. I remained in my office all day, alone with my fears. But at the end of the day I saw the driver Usta Zinhum at the door of the administration building looking at me. I shook hands with him, and felt that I really loved this old man with his big potbelly.

※

The days passed as usual. In the mornings I worked in a room crowded with dusty files that piled ever higher and gradually crept toward me. In the evenings I played backgammon with my only friends, Hassanayn, Magid, and 'Abd al-Salam. We preferred to meet at Masikh Café because it was on the main road between Dikhayla al-Bahariyya, the old neighborhood on the shore, and the newer South Dikhayla, which crept into the hills. The residents of both areas preferred their local cafés, and only passersby sat at Masikh Café. There were also a few young students who came to avoid the crowds, but because they saw that we were older, they never mixed with us.

I had met Hassanayn about a year earlier, after we both helped to save a girl from drowning. He said that he lived at Qabbari and had been coming to Dikhayla beach since his childhood, and that he used to have many friends in the area, but none of them were left except Magid, the pharmacist to whom he introduced me on the same day. They both talked a lot about their friend 'Abd al-Salam, who was in his tenth year in the army.

"You have been in Dikhayla for six years, and you don't know anybody?" Hassanayn asked me.

"I go to work and return home in silence. I don't meet anybody, and only rarely do I come to the beach," I replied.

He smiled and said, "There was a man like you on our street, who people thought worked for the intelligence."

Two months after we met, the war started. Magid was recruited into the reserve army. We later learned that he was behind the lines with the medical corps. I found myself worrying, together with Hassanayn, about 'Abd al-Salam, whom I had never met. We became even more worried when Magid returned at the end of the war, and we learned that 'Abd al-Salam was surrounded with the forces of the third army. When he returned, after the siege was over, I hugged him as though I really knew him. I told him that, since the beginning of the war, I had been having sexual dreams, and that one of them involved Golda Meir. He chuckled, but I swear I wasn't lying.

❈

Decorations filled the streets of Alexandria, so I knew that it was New Year's, but I didn't care. I buried both my marriage plans and my thoughts of selling the house. I didn't want to look out my windows because if I opened them I could be seen. There was no way out except committing a big robbery, and that was something I could not bring myself to do, or going to work in an oil country, which, because of my mother, I could not do either. But al-Dakruri, the thin pale representative of the workers' union, told me: "There will be two hundred workers this time, a large number, and you should know how to keep them under control. A pound and a half for each worker."

It was decided that on the twenty-sixth of July I should take them to Gamal 'Abd al-Nassir Avenue, near Sidi Gabir train station, where President Sadat was going to get off the special train on his way to Ma'mura. I stopped the two buses at the intersection of Saba' Banat Street and Haqqaniyya marketplace. I gave every worker one pound. It took a while for them to get off the buses, so the street filled with honking vehicles, and Manshiyya Square became a living hell. But everything ended well, and I gave fifteen pounds to Usta Zinhum, who had also been the driver on the previous trip, and another fifteen to the other driver, who was on his first trip with me. He laughed when he realized what we had done.

"No ratting," I said.

"No ratting."

"No ratting," they said, one after the other, and left happily.

My hopes were revived, but there was no news of any important visitor to Egypt this summer. I hid the seventy pounds in the mattress on which I slept, and they became a hundred when the shipyard gave us a bonus on the occasion of inaugurating a new ship. The summer passed quietly. On Fridays I met with Hassanayn and 'Abd al-Salam on the beach, but Magid had to work on Fridays. He always said that he dreamed of having his own pharmacy so he could take Friday off, and not Sundays, and that he was working hard to realize that dream.

We used to sit at Biso Bistro and watch the people around us. 'Abd al-Salam often talked of Dikhayla beach in the old days when it was clean and not crowded. There used to be foreigners living in the villas behind the courthouse, and they would hold musical and theatrical performances, as well as sports matches that were open to the public. Now the beach was neglected, and its visitors came from Qabbari and Mitras, bringing noise and arguments as well as cooking utensils and numerous children.

Hassanayn never stopped smiling and waving at the girls and women who passed by. Whenever he got a response, he blushed and said with embarrassment: "That's it for me. I can't go any further." We usually laughed at him, and only minutes later he'd resume his smiles and waves.

I often thought about the one hundred pounds, and, in moments of despair, repeatedly thought of wasting them. At the end of summer, winter arrived. One night at the café, Hassanayn asked me, "Why do you look so distracted these days?"

"On the contrary. I'm not distracted at all," I replied.

Magid said that many of his customers at the pharmacy forgot to pick up the medicine they'd bought, and then returned the next day to ask if they had forgotten anything. 'Abd al-Salam said that when he took the train to and from Rashid to go to work every day, he always saw people fighting as they got on and off the train, but once they were on the train, they remained as silent as deaf-mutes. I made up my mind to go to Holy Yahya, who sold carpets and straw mats as a street vender, for it was known that he was also a broker.

✻

"I will sell the house," I said to my mother one night, while I was wrapped in a rough blanket, reading the evening paper, whose headline was "Beirut Burning." We could hear the wind roaring and the rain beating on the houses and streets outside.

"Sell it, son," she replied, without looking at me. She was sitting in front of the kerosene stove warming up her hands as well as the small room where we sat. She had been awakened by the chickens screaming in the coop, which she had recently said she wanted to repair.

"I will rent a big apartment in the Bahari neighborhhood."

"Sell it, son," she repeated in the same tone. I could not tell whether it meant satisfaction or despair.

A few days later, Holy Yahya, who had decided to buy the house himself, came by. He brought along the fruit seller, 'Abdu al-Fakahani, who was building an apartment building by the sea, near the airport. Holy Yahya was the one who told me about 'Abdu, and said that he would put in a good word for me, so that I could rent an apartment in his building.

I made my mother put her fingerprint on a sales contract for a thousand pounds, which Holy Yahya paid in cash. It was the first time I had ever seen a thousand pounds. We were required to leave the house in six months. 'Abdu al-Fakahani wrote me a rent contract for an apartment that I was entitled to get in six months and took the thousand pounds. My mother remained silent and didn't stir the whole time. I felt my heart sink. Who is the winner here? I do have a contract, but it is no more than a piece of paper that, for any reason, may become useless. Holy Yahya has secured a house for himself, and al-Fakahani has received a thousand pounds! I could not retreat. If you had been as naive as I was, you wouldn't have retreated either. Besides, there is a kind of happiness that can suddenly swell up inside a person and make him very shortsighted indeed.

During the next four months, Holy Yahya visited us frequently, and I also went to see the apartment building and became less worried about my prospects.

"Why doesn't your mother sit with us?" Holy Yahya asked me on one of his visits. I couldn't find an answer. She hadn't been talking to me much. Every time a chick died, she brought it for me to see. If I was outside, she would wait for me to get home and see it, and I would hold it by its soft legs and throw it as far as I could out of the windows over the jam-packed rooftops.

"Her spirits will rise when you move to the new apartment," Holy Yahya said.

On my next visit to 'Abdu al-Fakahani, he said, "Mr. Shagara, I still have your thousand pounds if you want them back. The construction costs have gone up, and I need another two hundred pounds."

" . . . "

"Mr. Shagara, you are an employee in the big shipyard, and you can apply for a loan."

I left him, and didn't stop at the café. I had bought a kilo of oranges from him. I gave them to a beggar on my way home. It was only six o'clock when I got home, and my mother was already asleep. I heard the chickens clucking and thought of giving them some food. I had never done that before. Why do I dislike this peaceful house? What had gotten into me that I wanted to change something that has always been the way it is?

Lying on my bed, I felt weary, but I found myself thinking about my old Arabic teacher at the Ras al-Tin High School. He had a sad face and calm features. He always said that life was too short to be spent in sadness and worry. If you feel that way, all you had to do was get a sheet of paper and write a letter to whomever you had offended, or had offended you. Write to ask for forgiveness or to explain that you are hurt. You won't even need to mail this letter because you will feel better already, and will tear it up. My teacher said that this was his only successful method of getting rid of his worries and sadness. He disappeared suddenly from our school, and no one knew where he went, but many of the teachers became sulky and quiet after his disappearance.

In my utterly miserable state, I thought of writing a letter to my illiterate mother, who slept in the next room, asking for her forgiveness. I got out a sheet of paper, placed it on top of a newspaper, and laid it on my knee. I wrote:

> *Dear Mr. President, champion of the crossing and the victory: Please accept my sincerest greetings.*
>
> *We would like to inform Your Excellency that the workers of the Marine Vessels Shipyard have shown an enthusiastic desire to travel to Cairo to join you in the Labor Day celebrations. However, the Chairman of the Board objected, saying that this will slow down production. What production could be so important as to prevent us from expressing our love and support to Your Excellency?*
>
> *Sincerely yours,*
> *A faithful worker in the shipyard*

❋

At sunrise on the first of May, I was standing in front of two big buses at Masr Station. I felt the cool breeze on my face while I watched the rows of Peugeot taxis, their drivers smoking in silence. Usta Zinhum, who was on his third trip with me, was sleeping on the steering wheel, and so was Usta 'Abbas, who was on his second trip with me. The big broken station clock showed twelve o'clock, and there was little movement in the place. The station square had a large garden whose benches were occupied by sleepers covered in rags. I was smoking nervously, thinking about the week before and how I'd been overcome by hysterical laughter while playing backgammon with Hassanayn, Magid, and 'Abd al-Salam. I didn't want to tell them anything about this. Al-Dakruri had come into my office, looking even paler than usual.

"Prepare yourself for the Labor Day celebrations. I have recommended you because you know Cairo and Hilwan well."

It took a tremendous effort to keep my surprise from rising to my face. I had never visited either Cairo or Hilwan, and I was also trying to hide my anxiety long enough to find out the whole story. Al-Dakruri said that some cowardly worker had sent a letter to the president, claiming that the shipyard's chairman of the board was preventing the workers from traveling to join the President in celebrating their day. Al-Dakruri also mentioned that he was upset that the letter was written in terrible handwriting—I had used my left hand to write it, then mailed it from the main post office in Manshiyya.

The president's office had mailed the letter back to the shipyard with "We received this letter" written on it.

"So they haven't asked for anyone to travel to Cairo?"

He gave me a sarcastic smile, wished me a good trip, and left. I could hardly believe it.

I stood for a while watching the workers arrive, each carrying a small lunch bag even though the administration had promised to give them lunch and a bottle of the rare Spatis soda. The square bustled with movement as sunlight spread over the place and the ground glistened, still wet with dew. I was excited. The drivers of the Peugeot taxis were yelling: "Cairo, Cairo!" I was thinking of the two hundred workers. Each one was supposed to receive four pounds for the trip, but I was going to give them two. Out of the four-hundred-pound profit, I was going to give a hundred to each of the drivers and keep two hundred, which I could throw in the sly, pock-marked face of 'Abdu al-Fakahani.

A pleasant feeling of security came over me. I love this city, which drifts from winter into summer as if it were floating in an enchanted universe. There was not a single dark cloud in the sky. Only a few white clouds, like children strolling in the open space. Thank you, Lord, for not forsaking your son, Shagara Muhammad 'Ali, whose strange name has given him trouble during his childhood and youth, and is still distasteful to some of your impatient worshippers. Oh, Lord, please finish my act well, and don't disappoint me by killing my mother.

The two buses started down the road, which was shining with dew. The fog had lifted off the road but lingered in the fields to its sides. In a few spots, green trees appeared to be floating in a wide sea of white. There were many pigeons lazily hopping on the side of the road, but I was gazing at the tops of the casuarina and camphor trees looking for crows, ibix, or hoopoes. I could see that Usta Zinhum was looking at me and chuckling. We had decided to spend the day in Tanta. . .

3

*There is not a single person in Dikhayla who does not know Hajj
'Abd al-Tawwab. He owns the largest fleet of vehicles
trans-porting building stone from the mountain quarries. He is
a good man who goes on the pilgrimage every year and never
misses the 'Umra during Ragab and Ramadan. God granted him
a son after thirty years. One day, at the break of dawn, the people
were startled by the screams of his wife, who was running barefoot down the Mosque Street and jumping in the air. Since God
had granted him a son, it was the habit of Hajj 'Abd al-Tawwab
to spend most of his nights in prayer to God and repetitions of
His name. That night, he went on chanting, "Ya Latif, Ya Latif,"
not listening to the warnings of his wife. "Ya Latif" is one of the
names of God which has an immediate universal effect, or so said
one of the clergymen who later commented on the incident.*

*The ceiling of the room was cleft in two, and down came a
large radiant white bird, which filled the room with a bluish
glow. The bird took the boy to its chest, wrapped its feet around
him, and flew through the ceiling and open sky to the seventh
heaven, where the throne of God stands.*

Today is the eighteenth of June, a bland day without any celebrations, decorations, or speeches. For a long time, the twenty-third of December overshadowed the eighteenth of June. Then came the fifth of June to send them both to hell. Now the sixth of October is supreme. For the hundredth time, I could not keep myself from looking over the four large rooms, the wide living room, the oil-painted walls, the beige tiled floors, and the bathroom with its rose tiles, big bathtub, and movable shower head... I am getting taller...!

'Abdu al-Fakahani had finally given me the apartment after taking me to the verge of despair. Less than a week after he had received the two hundred pounds he told me that he needed another hundred. I screamed, and it was a comical scene, with me angrily waving my hands in front of his face, our heads only half a meter apart, as I struggled to restrain myself from hitting him. He walked away and sat down, while I kept pacing back and forth in his store, looking at the fruits and vegetables and thinking that I would like to pile it all on top of him until he died.

"I'm not rushing you. The apartment can wait."

I wanted to say that my mother would die if she heard this, but he looked as if he knew that. He was smiling like a monkey while I was about to explode. I could not even say a word, but something in the way I looked must have urged him to say: "You can write an IOU for the amount, and I can use it to borrow the money from another merchant."

I agreed. It was either that or I would kill him. No middle ground. He gave me the keys to the apartment, even before the scheduled date, and was shameless enough to congratulate me and wish me good luck. I thought of asking Magid, Hassanayn, and 'Abd al-Salam to help me move, but ended up renting a truck, and, in the middle of the night, I piled up all the furniture into it myself.

I heard my mother mumble "Bismillah" as she entered the apartment with her right foot, not forgetting to make sure that I did the same. I thanked God, thinking that she was going to like the apartment. I quickly put the old furniture in two rooms. The apartment looked as if it could accommodate all the furniture that I had seen displayed at stores on the streets of al-'Attarin, Tawfik, Salah Salim, and Fuad. I had seen these stores many times before, but only recently did I look at them more closely. I spent a whole week looking at furniture I knew I could not afford. But I did it when I was feeling optimistic following a pleasant surprise.

A few days after Labor Day, the chairman of the board of directors had called me to his office, and said, "You have honored us, Shagara."

He was a big man with a white face and rosy cheeks, and at that moment he had a big smile on his face. I would not have believed my eyes had it not been for al-Dakruri, who was also there, looking absolutely delighted.

"You have indeed honored us," he went on saying, and produced a thank-you note addressed to him and to all the workers who had participated in the Labor Day celebrations in Hilwan.

"It is a letter from the President's office. You will be famous, Shagara," he said, looking straight at me, but I was unable to utter a word. He must have thought that I was too happy for words, and decided to give me a raise. Al-Dakruri looked as if his face were going to burst with joy, but I just stood there in shock at how things worked in this country. . .

※

I went to the beach, where there were quite a few people. I was hoping to meet Magid, Hassanayn, and 'Abd al-Salam, but they didn't show up, so I sat alone at Biso Bistro. Most of the faces there looked familiar, but I didn't really know anyone. It was the early afternoon and I had eaten two Bolti fish, which I had grilled myself for lunch. My mother said that she was not going to eat until late afternoon, and remained sitting on the balcony, looking at the sea. I watched the children playing in the water and on the beach, the little girls walking together with their arms wrapped around each other's waists. I watched a few families who had gathered to eat under the umbrellas. The sun was shining brightly, flooding everything around me in waves of light, while my mother still wore her black mourning clothes. She inspires silence at home and sometimes even scares me. The silver paint on the walls makes her clothes look even darker, especially now that the electric light is brighter. Yesterday she said that she heard a noise in the apartment next door, so she went over and knocked on the door. A young man opened the door and she offered him her congratulations on the new apartment, but he laughed, and said that he was only a painter, and that most of the apartments in the building were empty because the renters worked in the Gulf countries. Then he asked her when we had returned from Saudi Arabia. He also asked if she liked the paint job in our apartment, and she said that she did.

"Does the situation bother you?" I asked her, and added, "I won't go to the café as often from now on." But she said that she was happy, and that she liked to spend the day watching the children on the beach nearby, the people who fish on the rocks in front of the building, and the ships moving in the sea. Then she smiled and said that she had never seen a ship before, and asked me why ships were so big and white.

Has any man in this world ever wished that he were born a girl? I have. Maybe if I were a girl, my mother would have been less lonely. She will never forget my father, Muhammad 'Ali Shagara, that kind, down-to-earth man. He married her when she was fourteen and patiently lived with her for twenty years until she became pregnant with me.

"You should name him," she said.

"Shagara," he said. She laughed, but he went on saying: "Shagara Muhammad 'Ali. I planted him ages ago. He will live as long as an olive tree, and will be as tall as a palm." He also said that his grandfather had been given that name, because he was born under a sweet-smelling camphor tree. Then he laughed and cried. He had become a father after waiting for twenty years.

I grew up with amazing speed at our old house in the Baladiyya housing project at Kum al-Shuqafa. My mother stopped telling me the story of my name and I stopped asking her about it, but continued to defend it in front of the other children, who teased me. I never complained. I was growing taller than all the others, and I used to think that when I grew up, I would be a real tree, that I would grow branches and leaves, that birds would land on me, and kids would throw pebbles at them. That thought both scared me and made me laugh. Suddenly, I became taller than my father, and became embarrassed of walking with him or with my mother, but he would always look at me and say, "Just as I had hoped."

I used to play in the alleys between the huge brick buildings, which stood in the middle of a large vacant lot surrounded by fields of bright green grass, with asphalt roads running between them all. No strangers came to our neighborhood, and no cars passed there. Mothers felt safe letting their children go out to play. What charm God had sent to this spot. He must have created it for Himself, and so filled it with peace and quiet. And He must have liked us, and so left it for us. It was always flooded with sunlight, in both summer and winter. Even though there was a hospital for pulmonary diseases nearby, we only saw the trees surrounding it and were not afraid. The days passed, as peaceful as a mother's pats on the head of her child. My father's small salary from his job as supervisor in the town workshop was enough for everything we wanted.

Bab al-Muluk was the commercial street. My mother and her neighbors bought leftover pieces of cloth from the Clock Square in Karmuz for themselves and their husbands and bought new clothes for us children. They would make joyous trips to Bayyasa to buy meat and seafood. We used to eat the shrimp like peanuts. Sardines were salted in the summer for the winter. We children enjoyed teasing the crabs with little wooden sticks.

On the day of 'Eid al-Adha, the men used to go to the nearby sheep market in the Tubgiyya hills to buy lambs and goats. The women dressed in black and went to visit the dead at the 'Amud al-Sawari cemetery. I can still smell the narrow alleys that we used to cross to get to Bab al-Muluk, the soapy water dumped from the windows onto the streets, and the sheep in the hills. I can still hear the gossip of the one-eyed broker. My father once said that, every morning before going to the market, the broker swore never to tell the truth all day. "This is how all brokers are, my son. Their only pledge is to lie!" my father said. I can still see the crowds at Bayyasa laughing and arguing, the women giggling obscenely as the mutton sellers pointed the sheep's balls at them.

But one day the whole place changed. The vacant lot became a field for soldiers training to use artillery. Barricades and anti-aircraft guns were everywhere. I came home one afternoon and said happily, "They gave us a holiday, because of Eden."

"Damn Eden, and these bad times," said my mother.

Later that day, my mother caught me with Kawthar, Hani's sister. I was not a little boy anymore. I was ten and was kissing Kawthar behind one of the doors. Kawthar always smelled nice and her blond hair hung loosely over her shoulders. She often came to visit our apartment. All the children were welcome in any of the apartments at any time. The doors were usually open, and stray cats went in and out as well. I was especially welcome in the neighbors' apartments because I was dark and my parents were both very white. That day I found myself moving closer to smell Kawthar's scent, and I didn't leave it at that. My mother slapped me for the first and last time that I can remember. I was her only son. She kicked me out of the house, so I went down to watch the soldiers who were standing by the anti-aircraft guns, constantly watching for any airplanes that might appear among the clouds.

As soon as the lot became vacant again, we went back to playing in it, with new memories. We played brave young soldiers firing anti-aircraft guns at airplanes that shone like distant stars. We had been brave during the actual war, and generous as well. We regularly offered food to the soldiers.

But things had changed. The grass was no longer soft and green. It was withered and patchy. The asphalt roads had lost their luster. The years went by in a dull monotony, and we soon became too old for games in the alley. My father started coughing.

"I have often found myself looking in the direction of the hospital," he said. "Now I know why."

My mother clapped her hand on her breast to show her shock.

"I can't help it," he said.

She crouched in a corner and wept. I realized that the hospital was more than tall trees, and that it had a door.

"How much have we saved?" he asked her.

I saw her pull out a small rolled-up cloth purse from inside the frame of their copper bed, and I noticed him looking at me. Twice I had had a strange fever strike me right before the final high-school exams and not pass until the exams were over. I was not a bad student, despite my occasional trips to the cinema with Hani and Rashid. Now Hani was in the military academy, Rashid in the school of medicine, while I was studying the same lessons for the third time, and fearful of another attack of the fever.

During the next week, my father bought a one-hundred-meter-square plot of land. He talked about Dikhayla and the hills where people bought cheap land. "If I die, you will have to leave this apartment," he said one day as a final statement on the matter. I had heard about Dikhayla before then, but had never seen it. I used to go halfway there, to the youth camp where high-school students went every year to practice shooting firearms.

The day after my father bought the land, exams were postponed, and a heat wave swept over the city together with strong *Khamasin* winds. Our neighborhood had already changed. Small piles of garbage had appeared everywhere, the garden seats were broken, and many of them disappeared. The trees around the hospital had lost most of their leaves and many of their branches, so that we could now see its windows and the patients who gazed out of them with lost expressions.

It seemed as though a gigantic black fist were gripping our world by the neck. Screams were heard on the streets. Women slapped their faces until they broke their teeth, and children huddled in corners to cry. President Gamal 'Abd al-Nassir had resigned, and the Israelis had entered the country.

We listened sadly to the stories of soldiers in ragged uniforms and bare feet who had taken to the streets, running away from death, from the Canal cities, where death was everywhere. We heard stories about the bodies being buried at 'Amud al-Sawari, coming from faraway hospitals. It seemed as if people had come to hate each other. They closed their doors at sunset, and darkness ruled the earth and skies.

I actually passed my high-school exams that year, but my grades were not good enough for me to go to college. I wasn't upset. I had no desire to learn anymore. I found a job in a new shipyard. I told my father that I would finish building our new house. He must have hated the hills after we moved there, because he didn't stay long. I hated the whole area, but where could I go? I learned that time was the best cure. The days passed meaninglessly. The area became more crowded, and children started playing in the dirty alleys around us. I learned that our desire for beauty is an acquired habit, and that we can become completely indifferent to our surroundings. I no longer hated the hills but came to feel indifferent toward them. I was even indifferent to the youth camp, which I used to notice on my way to work every day and remember how I had first learned to shoot, and how I used to stick a kerchief under my shirt to absorb the recoil of the Mauser gun. Even this camp lost its ability to attract my attention. I stopped looking at it. Only yesterday, I looked at it again to discover that the sign on its entrance had been replaced by another that said "Central Police Camp."

I thought that my mother had become as indifferent as I was, and it wasn't until it was too late that I realized she was more like my father. I took care of her faithfully, but it was useless. Those who say that children can make a woman forget about her deceased husband are liars. She never forgot Muhammad 'Ali Shagara, who disappointed me when I wanted to put some joy into his bleeding chest. Now she was doing it again, leaving me alone and going away with the white ships. . . I must be the one who killed her. I took her from the grim hills to the wide-open universe, and when she couldn't find other neighbors in the building, and couldn't go out because this damned apartment is on such a high floor, she took off into the universe. She shouldn't have done that. She was my mother. How could she leave me alone in this apartment with the bare walls? What woman would brighten up this dismal place? And how could I find her?

4

Fayyad, who worked in the oxygen preparation station at the shipyard, has now become famous all over Alexandria. He climbed a light tower, thirty meters high, and didn't come down. During the day he chanted the call to prayer several times, and the workers left their jobs to go watch him. The security officers came and called to him, but he did not respond. One of them tried to climb up to him, but discovered that it was impossible, and that Fayyad had a thick club in his hand. The shipyard manager came and called to him. Still he did not respond. They left him until the next day, and then brought his wife and three children and gave them a megaphone to call to him. Still he did not respond. His wife was a beautiful blonde in rags. At first everyone felt sorry for her, then they lusted after her. They fired shots near the tower, but he did not stir. They left him until the third day, and left his wife and children to sleep under the tower. Then the police and the firemen came, and climbed up to him from all directions, so he took out a knife, and slit his own throat.

Near the end of the year, winter takes hold of Alexandria. Thick black clouds form in the sky, and two storms hit, one after the other. By mid-January, the city is usually soaked in rainwater, and the sun timidly starts to appear. Slowly, it becomes sunnier and sunnier.

People reappear on the streets and tell stories about the rain that penetrated the roof, the wind that broke the window, and the influenza that attacked every member of the family. They talk about how much sugar cane they chewed, how much lemon and orange juice they drank, and how many onions and beans they ate. And there are tales of the electricity that went out, the thunder that frightened the children, the lightning that could be seen through the shutters, the heartless man who kicked his wife out on a cold rainy night and threw her clothes out the window, and the little girl who was standing on the balcony and was carried away into the street by the wind.

Women appear on their balconies, hanging out their wet clothes or just sunning themselves, and the city looks as if she had never endured those short gloomy winter days. The city is like a little child who screams in the shower, but as soon as it's over and her mother lets her go, she fills the house with joy and laughter.

But I went through that winter on my knees. I hated the year '76, that year that seemed like an extension of '67. Those two dirty digits had collaborated against me twice—the first time they took my father from me, and the second, my mother. My mother's death seemed like a divine punishment, but what could I have done? I only wanted to move a step up. Is there anyone who does not want that?

I often thought of Hassanayn, Magid, and 'Abd al-Salam, who rarely visited me. They came over once on the day after my mother died. I went to Hassanayn's house to ask for his help, and he brought them along. Despite our deep friendship, we had never visited each other at home. We always met at the café. My friends weren't ignoring me. They just hated houses and walls. Then again, perhaps the seed of our separation was always there, despite our apparent harmony.

I bought a 16" television set on credit after borrowing two months' salary from the shipyard for the down payment. I didn't give much thought to my debt to 'Abdu al-Fakahani, who came to my mother's funeral and told me that he didn't want the money right away. I didn't regret turning down the offer to participate in the twenty-sixth of July celebrations. They came less than a month after my mother's death. Al-Dakruri told me at the funeral that he could handle it by himself. I was afraid that the workers would ask him to do what I had done and that he would find out about my scheme. At the time, however, my sadness outweighed my fear, and I forgot to consider this possibility. I later learned that it all went well. I thought that perhaps he did what I had done, and that it had become his own secret. In fact, I came to like al-Dakruri, that thin and pale man. On the day my mother died, he brought me an authorization to let the shipyard and the union pay for the costs of her funeral.

❈

Yesterday I went to the café and, despite the cold weather, I found all of them there. Hassanayn laughed and said, "I told you he would come."

Magid and 'Abd al-Salam laughed too as they warmly shook hands with me.

"We all function according to a secret clock," Hassanayn went on after hugging me.

"Thank God that I moved into the apartment before the latest price hike," I said, "or al-Fakahani might have asked for yet another two hundred pounds." We all laughed.

"People are talking about nothing but this strange price hike, and they are so irritable, almost ready to fight thin air," Magid said. We remained silent for a few minutes and then 'Abd al-Salam said, "Funny we should talk about such public matters, when we haven't met in so long. We were talking about the same subject before Shagara arrived."

"Is there nothing new with any of us?" asked Hassanayn.

"You're right," 'Abd al-Salam replied in a voice that sounded like a deep sigh. "There isn't." Then he turned to me and said, "I'll tell you something that I hope won't upset you."

He told me that a few days ago he heard Holy Yahya at the bus stop explaining to someone how he makes money out of nothing. He said he bought old houses for 'Abdu al-Fakahani and that a year ago he bought one in the hills for him for a thousand pounds, which 'Abdu then sold for three thousand pounds a few days ago. He also said that he made handsome commissions on these sales, and that he was selling carpets and mats only as a façade.

I spent a maddening night. I felt like pounding my head with my own hands. I decided to kill them both—al-Fakahani, who sells rotten fruit, and Holy Yahya, who only inherited the title from his father, but has never actually seen Jerusalem, that short, stocky blond man with the red face and eyebrows, with arms as short as those of an insect and tiny hands. I bought a half-liter bottle of brandy and, drinking it for the first time in my life, I finished half of it. Then I slept like a dead man.

I got to work half an hour late. The administration offices were almost empty. Everyone was looking out the windows.

"The workers want to go out."

"Why are they preventing them? Maybe it would be better to let them go out, or else they may destroy the shipyard."

The workers' chanting could be heard like a loud roar from behind the tall wall surrounding their work stations. What is all this anger in the air? Finally the main gates were opened wide, and a flood of workers rushed out. Some of them ran toward the administration offices to try to convince us to join them. There were about a hundred thousand workers, maybe more. I knew from the files in my office that we only employed ten thousand. Dozens of them were carried on others' shoulders. I saw one with a white band around his head, madly waving a white handkerchief. He was attracting the most workers and was leading the whole demonstration.

"Who is he?" I asked the man standing next to me at the window, whom I noticed was remarkably overweight.

He laughed like an overjoyed child and said "You don't know him! It's Sayyid Birsho."

"Oh!" I say, trying to hide my smile and my inability to understand. I find myself forced to advance toward Sayyid Birsho and the flood of angry workers pouring down Maks Street. Traffic is blocked, and passengers stream out of the tram and stopped cars. The windows of the houses overlooking the street are thrown open, and faces of women and children appear in them. They're repeating the slogans, and I too am chanting along with Sayyid Birsho. I'm also looking carefully at the women's faces in the windows above, white flowers perched on the tops of tall trees. I can't hear their voices, because the roar of the workers is deafening, but I know from the movement of their lips and the waving of their arms that they're repeating the slogans.

The government has certainly been wrong to raise the prices of so many products. All these masses can't be wrong. But why am I not angry like they are? Why do the price increases not bother me, although I am hardly rich? Is it because I am single and on my own? Or because things happen in front of me, and I fail to notice them? A volcano is erupting around me, mountains are collapsing. "By hook or by crook, we will bring the government down. . . " What is Sayyid Birsho doing? "Who is in our parliament? Peasant thieves. . . " What is Sayyid Birsho saying? "Hey America, take your money back. Tomorrow the Arab people will crush you. . . " "The Zionists are on my land, and the Intelligence is at my door. . . " Sayyid Birsho isn't afraid. "Tell the sleeper in 'Abdin that the workers are hungry. . . " I look at Sayyid Birsho's face more closely, a fleeting image, at once both dark and pale. I catch sight of him, and I see the eyes of a ferocious wolf in his face—two sharp and piercing eyes. But they are also filled with tears. Are those tears that I see in his eyes or clouds of sadness? The workers take turns carrying him. He is small enough to be taken for a fourteen-year-old. All the slogans are his or a variation on what he yells.

Then the crowd's movement, already at a crawl, slows down further. Maks Street is becoming too small for the flood. Sayyid Birsho signals everyone to stop. The other workers who are lifted on the shoulders of the crowd signal too. He enters a side alley with a large mob of workers. I am among this mob. Everything appears unbelievably well planned. Now we are in front of the Bata shoe factory. Hassanayn works here. Will I see him?

"The free workers of the shipyard call the honest workers of Bata." What if I see him? What if he sees me? Most of Bata's workers are women and young girls. I know that. Here they are, looking out of the windows, chanting with us. I'm not chanting now. Where is Hassanayn? What does he do with all these hundreds of women around him? He must have to keep his eyes lowered all day long. I smile at the thought. "Long live the struggle of the Egyptian women. . . " Sayyid Birsho is mad. Now I'm chanting with him. I wish I could distinguish my voice in the din of the crowd. Some officials come out to negotiate with Sayyid Birsho. He shouts more slogans and refuses to negotiate. Suddenly I laugh at how tall I am. I feel, and I don't know why just now, like Gulliver in the Land of Lilliput. Then the doors open, and a flood of men and women pour out of them. The two crowds mix. I worry about how to avoid rubbing against the girls in this crushing crowd. If only I could see Hassanayn. Our group is turning around to join the rest of the demonstration. It's impossible for me to see Hassanayn. It's impossible for anyone to recognize anyone else in this crowd. My God! Is this really our demonstration? Now it extends as far as I can see. The workers of the cement factory, the oil and chemicals factory, and the leather tanneries at Maks, the Valley of the Moon, and Dikhayla have joined in. This must be Resurrection Day! We advance further, and my height annoys me because it almost makes me trip several times. I feel the cold air above us. "You who rule us with the police. The whole people can feel your oppression. . . " I shout after Sayyid, looking at the high windows.

We arrive at al-Tarikh Bridge and discover that the huge demonstration has organized itself. The men are in the front. Now it will be Resurrection Day! The cotton ginners are blocking the side streets—an infinite number of men and women in

rags and bare feet. On the bridge, the Central Police are form-
ing a thick wall, blocking the far end. They raise their bamboo
sticks in the air and hold their shields in front of them. There
are numerous boxes filled with tear gas canisters at their feet.
The voices of police chiefs are heard from behind them,
shouting into megaphones and asking us to disperse before we
expose ourselves to danger. The whole thing seems funny. Our
demonstration actually stops, following a signal from Sayyid
Birsho, who is still up on somebody's shoulders. He moves as
if he were on the back of a trained dancing horse, as if he were
swimming on a series of synchronized waves. The air is
becoming very cold, coming in from the port on our left and
slapping our faces. The little kiosk shop at the bridge entrance
is closed, and the blare of a radio is coming from inside. A popular Shadia song is on the radio. Shadia's voice is very beautiful.
The owner must have closed down in a hurry. "They dress in
the latest fashion. We live ten to every room. . . " We chant after
Sayyid Birsho. A long time passes. We don't cross the bridge,
nor do the Central Police advance towards us. It's very strange.
Sayyid Birsho shouts some greetings to the Central Police.

"What a guy!"

"Who is he?"

"That's Sayyid Birsho. Don't you know him?"

The voices are coming from behind me. Sayyid Birsho is
advancing while Muhammad Qandil sings on the imprisoned
radio: "Hey beautiful, say good morning, hey beautiful, look
at me. . . " I am determined to follow Sayyid Birsho. The tear
gas canisters explode in our faces and blue smoke fills the air.
Many are dispersed in the alleys of Kafr 'Ashri, but the main
body of demonstrators remains strong, inching forward, the
bridge shaking under our feet. The bamboo sticks sink into

40

our bodies as we plunge into the wall of policemen. One of them attacks me. He is not taller than I am, but the stick raised above me makes him a giant, a vulture on the attack from a mountaintop. I catch the stick with my left arm, bend down, and lift him up between his legs. I find him light as a feather, and maybe because I am right next to the railing, I find myself throwing him in Mahmudiyya Canal. I hear his body splash into the stagnant dirty water.

It is as though I have found the answer. We are a huge number, and the policemen have no choice but to flee. Every dozen or so of us are carrying one of them and throwing him into the stinking water, causing the rest to run and hide in the streets of Basal Port. Our flood advances to Saba' Banat Street, moving away from the old bridge—God only knows how it withstood all this.

I'm now at quite a distance from Sayyid Birsho, trying to push through the crowds with my shoulder and arms in order to get closer to him. What kind of jinni is he who has not fallen or stopped chanting? My height allows me to see that the stores on both sides of the street are closed. There is a single deserted tram on the street, the windows of which were smashed by the demonstrators as they passed. I hear Sayyid Birsho forbidding such acts of destruction. His voice is now clear to me because I'm close enough to him. The demonstrators burned down Labban police station after passing it and finding it surrounded by the Central Police. Once again, I catch myself looking at the high windows where there are still more pretty women and girls.

Then Manshiyya Square opens before us, and there's a chilly draft, and large mobs coming from the direction of 'Urabi Square. They are students from the school of engineering, the school of arts and letters, commerce, law, the whole university, as I learn from bits and pieces of conversation flying around me. "We, the students and the workers, against the capitalist coalition. . . " I chant more slogans after Sayyid Birsho, and see the happiness on the faces around me as we read the approaching signs: "Long Live the Struggle of the Students and the Workers." The phrase is on signs everywhere and it sounds like all hell has broken loose and everything is going to burn to the ground. It's a mad uproar, as though we're in the middle of thunder and earthquakes. Even the buildings seem as if shocked into complete stillness. We're not scared by the Central Police trucks coming toward us from Tawfik Street, against traffic, or from Salah Salim, Nasr, or the Corniche. Nor are we scared by the ones blocking the side streets and alleys or the huge number of policemen jumping out of the trucks to surround us. This is an empty gesture, for we own the ground and space of both Manshiyya and 'Urabi Squares. We fill the parks and the roads and our roaring fills the air like a tempest. The spontaneous order imposed by Saba' Banat Street, and then by Maks Street, is disrupted, and it becomes impossible to tell the workers from the students or separate the men from the women. I find myself next to two girls, and think that I should move away, but one of them looks at me and says:

"God! Why are you so tall?" Then she smiles at me and at her colleague. I don't know how to answer. I'm truly flustered.

"The bastards have started to attack!" she cries, and her eyes gleam with ferocity for a minute, after which I can't see her anymore. Feet trample bodies, and there are lions' roars and pigeons' squeaks as stones fly. Blue smoke covers everything, and buckshots tear into clothes and flesh. But in the end the square clears to reveal us, just as we have been before, angry in joy, ecstatic with the cold and the adventure. I feel fresh blood pouring into my veins. The wind is whistling above my head and banners are fluttering. I see policemen running away down the alleys, chased by small groups of demonstrators. They look pathetic. I remember the girl who spoke to me earlier, and smile.

I'm not sure how the old building, which had served as the Socialist Union for a while before it returned to its original function as the Stock Market, burned down, how the demonstration divided into two, one going down Chamber of Commerce Street and the other going along the coast, or why I joined the one on the coast. It must have been because Sayyid Birsho was at its front. We meet with more large groups of students, who join us. I don't know where we were heading. The sea breeze is strong and loaded with water, which sprays in our faces and sets us running and laughing, making our army stretch forward. Nassar's Restaurant, and others like Mustafa Darwish, Atheneus, the Louvre Café, and Mon Signor, are all burned down. Where did all the stones we tossed at the poor policemen come from? How did the tiles of the sidewalks come loose so easily, as if they had been placed there only to wait for us? How did it get to be four o'clock? How did I escape from the fire and smoke at Raml Station, in front of the Sidi Ibrahim Mosque, at Silsila and Shatbi? I approach Sidi Gabir Station alone. Did I lose them, or did they lose me? Was I with them, or did I walk alone half the way? How did Sayyid Birsho disappear and get away from me? I remember hearing someone giving an order to return to Manshiyya, and another ordering us to take shelter at the university. I do not remember paying any attention to either one. By then my feet were taking me away. The streets around me are empty of both vehicles and pedestrians. There's a burned bus on Gamal 'Abd al-Nassir Street and a burned tram at the station. Now I'm considering going home. I remember that a train leaves Misr Station in the evening going to 'Amriyya. It passes Sidi Gabir Station, then goes around Alexandria to Muharram Bey Station, Qabbari, Maks, and then into the desert. I have known that since I came to live in Dikhayla. That would be my only commute, and from Maks, I would walk to Dikhayla.

※

I was exhausted when I arrived at the station. The large parking lot in front of it was empty. The station itself was empty, no passengers, workers, or guards. Only iron windows, iron doors, and the cold grim English decor of the walls. I sat alone on a cold wooden bench whose smoothness made it even colder. I was surprised to feel a strange sexual excitement. If I were the one leading these thousands in an official rally, how much money would I have made? I looked around the station. The cold felt different from the cold of the morning. It was piercing, and I could almost see the icy air blowing madly, causing paper scraps to fly over the tracks. The cold empty tracks seemed to extend infinitely, and the few trees around me were bare. I could see only the back of a man far away, dressed in black and urinating against a wall. The place was quickly getting dark. This is really winter, and this is what traveling is like. I put my tired head between my hands and stretched my legs, surrendering to terrible exhaustion and fierce hunger, waiting for a train that might never come. Then I broke into tears, weeping with a sound that resembled a roar.

5

A teacher who had been sent to work in Sharjah returned home.
His telegram to his family had not yet arrived. He opened the
door of his apartment at night, and stepped in quietly to surprise
his wife and two children. He opened his bedroom door to find
his wife under a man. She looked at him, and he looked at her.
He quietly retreated. His feet found the door to the apartment as
he walked backward. He went out and down the stairs backward
as well. He went backward into the street, and walked backward
down the road. Everyone who saw him confusedly made room
for him to pass. His children, who had appeared out of one of the
alleys, followed him. They looked at him, and he looked at them.
He stretched his hands out to them. They stretched their hands
out to him. He could neither stop nor walk in their direction, and
every time they caught his hands, they slipped away again, the
children crying incessantly. All of Alexandria came to know him.
People stepped out of his way, traffic lights and vehicles yielded
to him. The man and his children disappeared and people almost
forgot about them, but I had a dream about him: he was in space,
orbiting around the earth, his children orbiting around the moon.

In winter, when raucous air flows down the roads, blowing paper scraps and screaming through the alleys, when the lights are turned off and you cannot tell the land from the sea, and the café becomes cold and wet, we all, without any prior agreement, refrain from going out. On the warmer nights we meet, also without any prior agreement. We go out at around the same time, and slowly walk down the side streets by the old walls, whose colors have faded. One of us may run into another, and we both smile, shake hands, and walk to the café together. Didn't Hassanayn say that we all functioned according to a secret clock? This has become an established rule, and sometimes we manage to meet by chance at other times, too.

This evening, we weren't playing backgammon. We had met early and sat close to each other, our eyes fixed on the television set, which was placed on a high shelf on the wall.

"The official rallies will start again, Shagara," Hassanayn said.

"I'll find an excuse for staying out of them," I answered.

"But why don't you participate. Do you think that what happened to you at the beginning of the year will happen again?" 'Abd al-Salam said, referring to the fact that I'd been arrested after the workers' demonstrations last January, an incident which had really rattled me. I had only been released because of the testimony of the chairman of the shipyard's board of directors who had said, "Yes, Shagara is usually assigned to lead demonstrations, as I told you, but they are official government rallies that the shipyard arranges to welcome the president and his guests."

I had almost shouted out that I was really the one who incited all the demonstrators, that I was the one who pulled up the lamp posts, tore out the sidewalk tiles, burned transportation vehicles, night clubs, and police departments. I don't lead official rallies, as he said, but only cheat, and I've never even gone to any of them.

They had arrested me at dawn, policemen lined up on the stairs from the street to the roof. I'm not sure how they opened the door to the building where I'm the only resident, since I always lock it at night. I suppressed my anger and rage. They also released me at dawn. I looked around the calm Pharaohs' neighborhood, where I had never walked before. Who would have guessed that the State Security office was in this beautiful neighborhood? There were many trees, some bare, some tall, some well trimmed. The streets had been washed by both the rain and the city cleaners. There were yards and fences around the houses.

It had been bitter cold, and the sky was threatening me with small drops of rain. I'd walked with my hands in my pockets. I don't like suits. I don't think that I'll ever wear a suit except on my wedding day, and I don't think that I will wear it again after that. I tried to keep my face covered with my upper arm. I saw Alexandria asleep for the first time. The city was relaxed, sighing peacefully, unaware of everything around it.

Over the next few days, I'd found excuses to avoid participating in the sweeping rallies of support for the regime, which poured out from every governorate in Egypt to 'Abdin Palace. Al-Dakruri led the workers. It was his second time after the last July 26th. He said that this would be my chance to prove what the chairman of the board had said about me. I realized that he did his job fully, and that my secret was still unknown. I said that I would wait until a year had passed since my mother's death. He seemed to respect my wish. On the first of May, it was decided that only members of the workers' union would go to celebrate Labor Day in Cairo. On the twenty-sixth of July the President flew to Alexandria in a helicopter, and so the welcoming rallies were canceled. It was as if they knew that I had no appetite for them.

In fact, I felt devastated. I remembered my decision to kill 'Abdu al-Fakahani and felt a strange fear. I had come to feel that I wanted to escape from everybody. I even went to see 'Abdu and asked him to give me until the end of the year to pay my debt, and he agreed right away. He too seemed to be afraid of me, I don't know why.

I ran into Holy Yahya on the street, and went to shake hands with him, but he walked away. I called him, shook his hand, and patted him on the shoulder. His red face had turned yellow, so I eased his anxiety, and said that someday I would need some carpets.

"I'm at your disposal," he said.

※

"That's Jerusalem airport," Hassanayn said, when the television began its live broadcast from there. Magid lit a cigarette. 'Abd al-Salam became very pale.

"Begin!"

"Dayan!"

"And Golda. . . look at her."

The comments were made by other people in the café. We all fall silent when the door to the airplane opens. There is President Sadat himself, his smile wide as he shakes hands with the Israeli leaders. He smiles widely as he shakes hands with Golda, and warmly spends a few moments shaking Dayan's hand. His teeth are bright white and his mustache neatly trimmed. I thought of the wide street behind us, how empty it was now, and of the silence that had fallen over the people living in the hills. Silence and gloom were filling the space behind me as darkness fell. I was sitting on the edge of a cliff over a deep valley. One push backward would have left me dead.

"A soft, sly melody, like the groan of helpless, defeated souls," 'Abd al-Salam said, commenting on the Israeli national anthem. Then he got up, stuck his hands in his pockets, and paced around us, looking at the ground. The electricity went out.

"Good," said Magid with trembling lips. We didn't leave the café. We sat by the light of the candles brought by Muhsin, the waiter who rarely spoke.

"How can he do that?" Magid asked as if he were talking to himself. He took off his glasses and started wiping them with his handkerchief. I wanted to joke about it, and so said to Hassanayn:

"Here he has finished you off with a single trip." He smiled and blushed. It was not a full smile. Neither Magid nor Hassanayn laughed. 'Abd al-Salam walked away from us and slowly wandered into the dark street. Whatever I said seemed silly. I suppose I was getting into politics, unintentionally.

Hassanayn had once talked about himself. He said that he was a low-level employee waiting for a big financial windfall before getting married. He had failed regular school, but had managed to get his high school diploma through correspondence school. He became a correspondence student in the history department at the school of arts and letters. He didn't have enough time to learn about all the wars and conspiracies that seemed to make up most of human history. It took him two years to pass each year's exams. He also had asthma, not too serious, but it was still asthma. He laughed at his strange circumstances and said that he was the only person in the country who was fighting on all three fronts at the same time: poverty, ignorance, and disease.

"Just like the July 23rd Revolution," he added with a giggle. We all laughed too. He didn't seem embarrassed and remained cheerful.

I asked Muhsin, the waiter, to bring us a backgammon board. I was afraid that Magid and Hassanayn would let me down, but they both agreed to play. 'Abd al-Salam returned from the darkened street.

"*As-Salamu 'Alaykum*," he said, shook hands with each of us, and sat down, while we looked at one another. He greeted us as though he had just come in, as though he had not been sitting with us a few minutes before. He probably realized that his behavior seemed strange. Maybe he noticed our surprise as we shook hands with him. He sat in silence for a while then joined our backgammon game. When the electricity finally returned, we were the only customers in the café. The waiter didn't turn the television back on, and we didn't ask him to. We talked about the summer, and how we had not met then, and we asked Magid how his work was going at the pharmacy he was renting. He had finally fulfilled his dream of being self-employed. He said that setting up the pharmacy had kept him too busy to meet us, but that now he had more time, since he had hired another pharmacist to help him. 'Abd al-Salam told us about his father's health, which had deteriorated because of prostate trouble. He said that his father was getting better, and that the real problem was just old age.

"Of course you were busy planning to kill 'Abdu al-Fakahani and Holy Yahya," Hassanayn said, and we all laughed loudly. Then we asked Hassanayn why he hadn't come to the café in the summer.

"You weren't here," he said.

❋

"Of course you're bitter, because you fought in the wars twice," I said to 'Abd al-Salam on the road. We had left the café and it was almost midnight. We realized, a bit too late, that Hassanayn had left us and was waiting alone at the bus stop. A little while later, Magid entered his house on Mosque Street. As usual, I was left alone with 'Abd al-Salam. We lived on the same street. He lived in the middle, and I lived at the end, where it overlooks the sea.

We walked in silence, broken only by a distant stifled moan coming from the police department. I shivered in the November breeze. All the stores on both sides of the street were closed.

"No, I'm not," he finally answered.

We walked along, sometimes moving away from each other, then getting closer together again.

"What do you know about that villa on our street, the one surrounded by jasmine trees?" I asked him suddenly. I don't know why I chose to ask him at that particular moment.

"Have you seen anyone in it?" he asked. He knew what I wanted to talk about.

"Every day, in the early morning, I see a beautiful face looking out the window, a face as bright as light itself. Today, she waved at me." We returned to our silence. The street was uneven, and I almost tripped several times.

"Stay away from the house of jasmine."

I didn't understand. Something made me hesitate to ask him why, even though I wanted to. The scent of jasmine had attracted me ever since I had moved from the south of Alexandria to the north. The villa, standing behind high walls crowned with white and yellow flowers, seemed mysterious and magical. Its high round windows, its circular walls, its marble columns—everything about it seemed to have been made carefully and painstakingly. The face I saw in the mornings and evenings excited my imagination and curiosity, awakened my desire to get married. I could not confess any of this to 'Abd al-Salam.

"This house of jasmine is older than you or me," he said. "My mother and father and everyone else knows that. I was spanked repeatedly when I was a child for climbing that wall to pick a few jasmine flowers. The owner of the house and his wife prefer to remain isolated, and don't mix with anybody. They have only daughters—the most beautiful of all creatures. Everyone knows this, and only a lucky few have ever seen them. It may happen by chance. I don't believe you when you say that you see the girl's face every day. The man and his wife don't allow their daughters to go out into the street for school or work, and they don't let them stand at the windows, either. You may be lucky enough to see them once every so often in the very early morning—at dawn, before the man and his wife get up—but it rarely happens at night. Darkness enfolds the garden, the high windows are closed, and the thick blinds are pulled down, whether it's winter or summer. I had forgotten that the house was on our street, and I don't even smell the scent of jasmine anymore. Only once did I long for it, when I was trapped with the third army. Can you believe that? The air was full of the smell of smoke and gunpowder, and for a moment there, like a bright flash of light, I could smell jasmine. By God it happened, but only once. After I returned home, I watched the windows for a while, but I was not as lucky as you are, to catch even a glimpse of the only daughter left in the house. . . "

"How do you know all that?" I asked him at once, as if I could hardly wait for him to finish his last sentence.

"Secrets get revealed despite all efforts to conceal them. All of Dikhayla knows the secret of that house. A strange event occurs every few years. One of the girls suddenly arrives at the house in a taxi with a man in broad daylight, carrying a baby. It is the same taxi each time, and the same driver. She looks around for a few minutes before the iron gate opens for her, looks at the surrounding windows and balconies, as if to announce her arrival. That's how people know that one of the daughters was married the previous year."

"A strange family!" I said as if I were letting out a sigh.

"No one knows what's right and what's wrong," he said cryptically, and then stopped and held my hand. At that moment I was thinking that 'Abd al-Salam had his own secrets, and that I didn't really know him that well. A flock of white sheep came out of a side alley raising up a small cloud of dust. It was a strange sight at that time of night, and it seemed that the flock, which was now passing in front of us, was endless.

"Do you notice something?"

"Most of the sheep have three legs. Most of them limp."

"They all do."

I almost confessed that I was frightened. 'Abd al-Salam said that he felt that he was going to throw up. The flock came to an end, and a man appeared behind it, his body and neck bundled in several layers of clothes.

"He also has one leg, and is hopping with a cane."

I was covered in sweat and found that 'Abd al-Salam was leaning heavily on my arm. We trudged along in complete silence. We were in the vacant lot that leads to our street and almost out of Dikhayla. My nose was racing ahead of me as usual to smell the jasmine. Then we stopped. There was a taxi, its headlights turned off, stopped in front of the villa. The iron gate opened and we saw her step out in a flowing white wedding dress that shimmered in the darkness. She wore a crown, whose gems were also glittering. At her side was an old man in a dark suit, and the whole world was silent. We saw the driver open the taxi door for them and watched as they entered through the gate. Then we heard the iron gate close, and the taxi quietly drove toward us down the uneven street. I didn't want to look at 'Abd al-Salam's face, and maybe he felt the same way. As soon as the taxi passed us, we both turned and saw her looking at us through the glass. Was she looking at me or at 'Abd al-Salam? Neither of us said a word.

A few minutes later, I found myself alone. How did I fail to notice my friend turning toward his house? Did he say good night to me, and I have forgotten? Why am I looking around as though I've lost something? I went up to my apartment and opened the window. My God! I hadn't even noticed the cold sea breeze at the entrance to the building!

I looked at the endless darkness and the faint light of a faraway ship. This ship has been anchored outside the harbor for a month now. I'm sure it is the same ship, although there haven't been any storms to prevent it from leaving. I listened to the sound of the waves—angry, content, or cowardly, I couldn't tell. What if I threw myself onto those solid rocks? Would I die? So be it. That stupid sea has been doing nothing except ebb and flow for millions of years, all by itself, refusing to share anything with anybody, indifferent to the ships riding it, the garbage dumped into it, or the fish fighting in its depths. Would the world even miss one of its forgotten creatures? But then I thought about the reception for the President when he returned from Jerusalem in a few days.

6

Suddenly, the people were talking of nothing except Shaykh Lashin, who gave the sermon at Friday prayers in the Sidi al-Qabbari Mosque. Every Friday, the mosque became as crowded as Mount 'Arafat on the day of the Hajj. People were packed in the streets and on the roofs of houses around the mosque. Everyone was attracted to the fiery sermons of the Shaykh, who talked about issues that were not usually part of the Friday sermon. It became known that Shaykh Lashin did not memorize the sermon dictated by the Ministry of Awqaf, and that he did not improvise either. He memorized his sermons out of books that were inaccessible to everyone else.

A few weeks ago, he ended his sermon with a prayer in which he said, "May God make the armies of the Muslims victorious over the armies of the Franks and the Tartars. May God support the Caliph of the Muslims, Al-Mustakfi Billah Suliman, and bless the 'Abbasids. May God aid our Sultan, Muhammad bin al-Malik al-Mansur Qalawun, and his soldiers. . ." and the crowds continue to come. . .

What inspired me to be so daring? Was it the mystery of the house of jasmine? Did I really hope to find the girl in the window? If that were true, then I was quite unlucky. If my mother's death were a punishment for my plans to get married, then my bad luck must have been a punishment for my mother's death. What vicious circle from hell is this? Perhaps that was why I hesitated. But as soon as the three buses arrived at Damanhur, I made them stop. I took Usta Zinhum aside, but he spoke before I could say anything: "I do not feel comfortable about it this time."

For a minute I was dumbfounded, then I said, "Neither do I, but let's go back, and come what may."

I signaled to the two other drivers to join us. Usta 'Abbas had done this with me before, but the third driver said, "You will take two pounds from the payment of each worker, and that makes eight hundred. Do you seriously intend to give each of us a hundred pounds and keep the whole five hundred for yourself?"

"So you're not against the plan in principle?"

"The money should be divided fairly."

"You will take the hundred pounds or nothing at all."

It was as if I had set myself on a suicidal course. A few of the workers were looking at us and laughing. Many of them had gone out with me before, and they were usually the ones who convinced the others. I gave each worker three pounds. The administration had decided to give them five each. When we arrived at Alexandria, the third driver took a hundred pounds, and left, laughing. I knew that he had realized that he had to accept what I gave him, and that he couldn't rat, because there were four hundred workers and two other drivers ready to deny that any of his claims were true.

In the evening, I went to see 'Abdu al-Fakahani.

"You bought my house, and sold it for three thousand pounds within the same year. You blackmailed me twice. I will not pay you anything more, and I will find a way to get back what I have already paid you," I said to him, then left. I imagined that I had a torch burning in my hand and was running with it like a madman, burning down houses and stores. He trotted behind me, and when he finally caught up, he stood in front of me, his head barely level with my chest, and stretched his arms out to block my way. A knock on the head would have scattered his brains. I was puzzled to see that he was smiling. We returned back to the shop, as people watched this strange scene.

"Who did you hear bought the house for three thousand pounds?" he asked me.

"Ahmad Karioka."

"Does he own two pennies to rub together? Do you really believe that? Besides, that was a long time ago. I haven't asked you to pay the two hundred pounds you owe me, and I have even torn up the IOU you wrote for me." He was smiling as he spoke very confidently. He reminded me that this Ahmad Karioka fixed kerosene stoves and probably didn't earn much these days.

"Mr. Shagara, it was indeed I who bought the house both times. Both Holy Yahya and Ahmad Karioka, and their like, are my puppets. Garbage."

"What exactly do you mean?"

"First, your house really wasn't worth more than a thousand pounds. Second, you work in a government office, and know nothing about what we do. And you'll find out in a few days anyway. Besides, I have rented out the rest of the apartments in your building for three thousand pounds each. So I was generous with you, and you may ask the rest of the tenants about it." His smile was getting wider as he spoke. I was almost standing on the tips of my toes.

"Ha!" I said. "All the renters are in the Gulf countries."

"Well, the oil will run out some day, and they will come back. Oil wells are not bottomless, and maybe there will be a war, and all hell will break loose. . . "

"Have you actually torn up the IOU?"

"As you wish!" He continued to smile. I threw the two hundred pounds in his face, and he pulled the IOU out of his pocket. As I grabbed it, I noticed that his fingernails were red. Then I left, and I don't know why but I felt like laughing.

❊

"How much is in your bank account now, Mr. Shagara?" The chairman of the board asked me after he stood up and came from behind his desk to stand in front of me. I looked at al-Dakruri, who looked like he had shrunk, standing by the desk and biting his lower lip.

"What account, sir? I don't have an account," I replied.

"You take half of what we decide to give the workers, and only take them halfway to their destination."

I felt like swallowing my saliva, but my mouth was dry. I didn't reply. He was moving closer to me as though he were about to slap me.

"And I got you out of your trouble with the police. I, who was a general in the army—and believe me, the Israelis never took me lightly! Now I discover that you have been cheating me. I will find a way to put you in jail." As he spoke, he made a full circle and went back to sitting behind his desk. I looked at him closely as he sat down. I was, in fact, astounded to hear what he said, but I noticed that he was looking down at the floor and had almost closed his eyes. I was amazed, but I realized that I would come out of this a winner.

"I am innocent, and I believe that you once received a thank-you letter for my efforts. Also, al-Dakruri has taken the workers out several times, and if what you say were true, he would have known it. Al-Dakruri, did you know about any of this?" Al-Dakruri didn't answer.

"The last trip was very difficult. No one received us, and we had to stand on the road to the airport by ourselves. It was a big mess, and nobody knows who really participates in the President's receptions anyway." I actually managed to go on saying all this. It must have been someone else saying it. Al-Dakruri's face had turned yellow, and I thought that he was going to disappear. My story about the road to the airport was based on pictures and headlines I had seen in the newspapers on the day following the President's return.

"Get out. Get out of my face!" the chairman yelled, so I left. Al-Dakruri ran after me and put his hand on my arm, but I pushed it away and ran in panic.

I kept the remaining three hundred pounds, in preparation for any punishment I might receive. Every man and woman working in the administration smiled at me or at the floor every time we met. So it became clear that the news had spread as quickly as the turning of the machines, and my disgrace was now complete. I discovered that most of the employees knew who I was, when I had thought that I was alone and anonymous in my office with only the files around me. The third driver came to swear to me that he had not said a word to anyone, and he offered to return the hundred pounds I had given him. I told him that I was the only one responsible for what had happened, and that if he expressed his thoughts to anybody, we would all get in trouble, and maybe all get fired. In the evening 'Abdu al-Fakahani stood in my way and said, laughing, "I sold the house for ten thousand pounds."

"Why should I care about that?" I asked.

"I told you that you would find out in a few days."

At that moment, if I had had his neck in my grip, I would have choked the life out of him.

"Did you sell it to yourself again?"

"No. This time I sold it to another merchant. I think you understand now."

❋

I confessed everything to Hassanayn, Magid, and 'Abd al-Salam. I hesitated at first. Maybe I just needed to get a load off my chest. I almost stopped in the middle of the story. I was afraid that they would understand nothing more than the basic facts—that I was a thief. But they only laughed. Maybe they were just trying to avoid hurting my feelings, but they kept laughing. They never criticized any of what I had done. Every night they asked me to repeat the story, and then laughed at it again. I said that although I shared their laughter, I felt afraid every day when I went to work. At the very least, the chairman could force me to pay back what I had taken of the workers' money. In that case, I would have no choice but to return the apartment to 'Abdu al-Fakahani and become homeless.

Hassanayn said that people quickly forgot scandals, and Magid said that there might even be some people who secretly approved of what I have done. Then Hassanayn reminded me that it had been two weeks since my meeting with the chairman, and that if he were planning to do anything about it, he would have done it by now.

❈

I opened my first bank account with the three hundred pounds. I couldn't believe my eyes when I read the news in the *Al-Ahram* newspaper on the bus one morning. I remembered our meeting, and how the chairman had seemed really shaken, even while he was threatening me. He must have known it then. The poor man!

"You're lucky, Shagara," said al-Dakruri when he came to my office later that afternoon. I hid my smile.

"The chairman of the board has been in a difficult situation since the January demonstrations. The national security police discovered that the shipyard was a communist den, and that there was no record of a worker named Sayyid Birsho, and by the way, they have not found him yet. This week, they arrested three workers who were affiliated with secret organizations."

"Did the chairman write a report about me? Does the new chairman know anything about it?"

He smiled and said, "No. I just came from a meeting with him. He invited me and the department managers to meet with him on his first day."

I'm saved, I thought, then said to al-Dakruri, "I will not take part in any more rallies."

I added forty pounds to the three hundred after we received a bonus of one month's salary on the occasion of inaugurating a new ship. A picture of the new ship appeared in the newspapers, with the new chairman standing next to it and smiling. Alexandria was blanketed in winter weather, so I didn't go out in the evening. I thought of visiting my mother as soon as the weather cleared. She was buried with my father in the cemetery of 'Amud al-Sawari, in a public graveyard for the people from the town of Dalgamon who had emigrated to Alexandria. I have never seen that town, but I know that it is in the al-Gharbiyya governorate, and that it is between Kafr al-Zayyat and Tanta, and was the home town of 'Umar Lutfi, founder of the cooperative movement in Egypt. When the weather cleared, I forgot about visiting my mother, maybe because I hate cemeteries.

At the café, Hassanayn said, "I heard rumors that the new chairman of the board was appointed to punish the workers."

"He said it himself in a general meeting! His first decision was to cancel the temporary exemption from military service, which used to be granted to technicians in the shipyard because it serves as a strategic resource. Now more than three thousand technicians have been drafted in one month. Production has dropped dramatically."

Magid was busy playing backgammon with 'Abd al-Salam. After pushing his glasses up on his nose, he said, "It isn't a matter of demonstrations. The shipyard was a Soviet project in the first place."

"Thank God that Bata is Italian!" Hassanayn joked, and we all laughed so loudly that we startled the people around us.

"If Bata were Soviet," Magid said, "they would have beaten all of you with shoes. They would have beaten you especially, Hassanayn. Look. Imagine it!" He started pointing at Hassanayn and pantomiming the scene in the air with his hands, while 'Abd al-Salam and I couldn't stop laughing. "You're standing in the middle of a crowd of soldiers. The soldiers are all barefoot, holding their shoes instead of guns. You're on your knees, blindfolded, and your hands are tied behind your back. Ready. . . Aim. . . Fire! The target is the July 23rd Revolution known as Hassanayn! Ready! Load! Beat!" We almost fell off our seats with laughter. Magid has the face of an innocent child. He seems serious most of the time, and if you thought about it, you would think that he was altogether too serious about most things. But, on the other hand, when he jokes he jokes with all his heart.

I got up and stretched my back, which was beginning to ache from all that laughing. The other customers were giggling at our hilarity, and so was the waiter, Muhsin, who almost never laughed, which made us laugh even harder. They say that Muhsin has been depressed since he got married. Three months after the marriage there were strange changes in the voice and body of his wife, who finally turned into a man!

"You were the one who described yourself as the July 23rd Revolution," 'Abd al-Salam said to Hassanayn, whose face had turned quite red. I found myself calmly asking Hassanayn, "By the way, why does your company make such ugly shoes?"

"A shortage of molds, Shagara," he replied. Magid was no longer sitting among us. He was bent over, holding his belly, and exploding with laughter. The strangers sitting around us were staring at the strange scene. I had deliberately asked the question seriously, and Hassanayn answered in the same manner. Both the question and the answer became a complete farce.

I'm indeed happy to have paid my debts, opened a bank account, ended the scandal, and escaped punishment. I had firmly decided to begin looking for a wife. Now it seemed impossible that I had been the cause of my mother's death or that God was punishing me. I had escaped many evils with ease, which meant that He was on my side. I thought of wandering around the branch administration offices, away from my office where I was besieged by files and dust, in order to sniff out members of the opposite sex. Now, sitting here at the café, I realized that I knew all the female employees in the administration offices, and that they were all either married or engaged. It had been five years since any new employees were hired, and it isn't reasonable to expect that a girl would stay unmarried for five years after she starts working. Furthermore, most of the female employees have been working for longer than that. After Magid sat back down, 'Abd al-Salam said, "We must be going crazy. All this laughing is unnatural."

"Why should we go so far?" asked Magid, struggling to keep from laughing further and wiping the tears from his eyes, having taken off his glasses. "Dr. Musa, who works with me at the pharmacy, is constantly swearing at the country and the people, and wondering why people never get well, and why the nation doesn't just kill them and get it over with. He also says that he will not rest until he has a chance to work abroad, specifically in Kuwait." Then he laughed again, and we struggled to restrain ourselves from joining in.

"You must be working with Dr. Hitler without knowing it," said Hassanayn, and this time we didn't laugh. 'Abd al-Salam said, "By the way, I have decided to go work in Iraq." We all fell strangely silent, as though we hadn't been laughing our hearts out only a few minutes earlier.

7

A baby was born with a tail—a perfectly ordinary event that could happen. A week later, Alexandria found out that it had happened again, and people started talking about it. Just one week later, it was rumored that a woman had had a third child with a tail, and it soon became known that Shatbi hospital was filled with newborn babies with tails. Every pregnant woman hoped for a miscarriage, and some of them died trying to abort themselves. It was said that the year was cursed, so people stopped getting married. Strong-willed men stopped making love to their wives, while the weaker ones sent their wives to their parents or divorced them until the end of the year.

"No sooner had I graduated from the school of agriculture than I was drafted into the army. I was dragged into defeat in my first war, and I was surrounded in the second. I was neither sad nor frustrated, but now that I'm out, I feel like I'm on one side and the rest of this universe which God created for us is on the other. Do you really think that I like backgammon or sitting at the café? Do you think that we'll keep doing this forever? If so, then the tragedy will be complete. The normal thing would be for us to separate, for each of us to go his own way, and make a life for himself, and for each of us to remember the others from time to time. Yet we can't, not because Dikhayla is so small—nothing more than one street and a few alleys—but because none of us has a purpose to his life. Do you know why Hassanayn insists on studying at his age? Don't tell me that it's to get a university degree. What is a degree worth in the age of people like 'Abdu al-Fakahani? In reality, it's because if Hassanayn doesn't study, he will find time to think about himself!

"And you. You have an apartment and you live alone and have no responsibilities. But you also don't want to get a life of your own. Why don't you get married, now that you have taken the most difficult step? Are you enjoying the life you're living? I don't think so, but I don't think it's too bad either. It's just bland. You must be aware of this, but unwilling to face it. The only one who has found a purpose to his life is Magid. Now he's the manager of his own pharmacy. Yet instead of making it serve a real purpose in his life—that is, to make it a base for further progress—it has become his life. He hides in it from the world, and rarely leaves.

"I'm just like the rest of you, or maybe worse. My days present no new challenges in which I can prove myself a winner or a loser, only a routine job in agricultural inspection in Rashid. I often feel too lazy to go to work. I sleep until noon, and my boss never questions me. If you ask me about agriculture, you'll discover that I have forgotten everything about it, but if you ask me about any other job, I will tell you that I'm only an agricultural engineer. None of us has been successful at anything, but we have not been failures either. We stand in a vacuum.

"Now I'm out of the army, and I don't like talking about my experiences there. I don't know how I survived. This is my final conclusion. I try to put an iron curtain between me and my past.

"I only failed with one person, a young soldier who joined the army five years after I did. I was drawn to his beautiful baby face and his calm soothing voice. I always felt that he was older than I was. He used to fill our trenches with stories from every time and place. He always had a new novel for you to read. I could hardly believe that he was a medical doctor. A few days before the war, he met with me alone after midnight and said that we had to meet after the war. 'I agree. After the war,' I said, with a smile. He said that he was not joking and that the war was going to begin in a few days. How did he know that? I, and thousands like me, were bored with the military drills and the waiting, but we didn't see a war coming. He was different from everyone I knew. He wasn't in contact with any authority which could inform him of the date of the war. He was just an ordinary soldier, and none of us knew anything about the war until it started. Even the officers didn't know about it, and the rest of the people must not have known about it either. You must have read about this in the newspapers. I asked him why he wanted us to meet after the war. He asked me in turn what I did on my days off. I said that I saw my parents, my brothers and sisters, played backgammon with my friends, and slept. He asked me what they talked about. I said that at the café, we only played backgammon, and at home everyone fought. He said that our life was lost between fighting and playing. The country itself was lost, and had to be saved. Then he said, in an amazingly casual manner, that he and I could do it, and that, of the hundreds that he met in the army, I was the only one fit for this mission.

"He said that we were going to conquer Israel, not because we were stronger, but because we were going to fight with a suicidal spirit. 'The trenches and the continuous drills make death part of daily life. We will fight because we will be ready to sacrifice ourselves. Suicide can also be an investment. This is what will happen,' he said, and once again added, 'in a few days.'

"I was shaking as I listened to him talk, and almost cried with him when he cried. I couldn't sleep that night, nor for several nights afterward. During the first few days of the war, the battles seemed to me like dreams. I was asleep as I crossed the Suez Canal, asleep as I ran on the sands of Sinai, and once I actually fell into a real sleep for a long time. It was during a big attack on our new position on the east bank of the canal. The raid ended and the dead were carried to the west bank while I was actually in a deep sleep. I haven't seen him since that day. I didn't shed a single tear, because soldiers don't cry. But the question has often tortured me: Am I really capable of leading a revolution in this country? And why? I don't personally feel that anyone else has a problem. Everyone I know manages somehow. I have often tried to define a goal for myself, but I can never find one. When I got out of the army, I realized that I was thirty-three years old, and that even the clothes and hairstyles had changed. Someone over thirty like me can't do anything, but you, you, Shagara, and Hassanayn and Magid, are really at fault, because you have had a real opportunity to keep track of the years as they passed by. You can think I'm crazy if you wish."

This was what 'Abd al-Salam said to me on the last night before he left for Iraq while the two of us were walking home together. We always passed by the house of jasmine and found it dark except for a faint light behind the windows. We fell silent, and I wondered what 'Abd al-Salam was thinking as he passed the house. Maybe he also wondered what I was thinking. After he left, I decided to always walk home on a parallel street and not pass by the house of jasmine again.

I thought that 'Abd al-Salam was like the thousands of young men who worked abroad to earn the money necessary for securing an apartment and getting married, but then I realized that this was not his goal. The modest means of his family didn't bother him either, for he never talked about that, explicitly or implicitly. At some point I thought that he was like Sayyid Birsho, but the sadness in his voice told me that he was different, a type of person that I have never been able to fully understand. In any case, he wasn't crazy. He was like the many young people who stand at the bus station, distracted and oblivious to the burning sun over their heads, unaware that if they moved a few steps they could be standing under an awning. I often noticed these people and caught myself at the bus station counting the people standing at a distance from the awning. Maybe 'Abd al-Salam was different from those people, too. The fact was that I couldn't understand him. I liked him even before we met, and I still like him. Magid received a letter from him and brought it to the café, so we learned that he had found a job in a place called Khalis, not far from Baghdad, on a greenhouse farm. We took down his address, and every time we met, we said that we should write back to him. Each one of us decided to write, but never did. It seemed that we only remembered him when we were together. Maybe we felt guilty, or felt like vindicating ourselves. The summer and winter had already passed.

On Labor Day, only the members of the workers' union went to the celebration, as they had the year before. On the twenty-sixth of July, the President came to Alexandria by helicopter, and so there were no reception ceremonies. It was said that the helicopter was a gift from President Nixon, which he had presented to President Sadat in 1974. How horrifying! Nixon gives the President a helicopter and puts an end to the ceremonies, my annual source of income. But I had decided not to go out with the workers anymore, so why should I be so frustrated?

Magid often seemed preoccupied, and on several occasions, I thought of asking him about it, but then I forgot. On the first of October, he cleared up the mystery, and said as if he were spellbound, "She is dark with green eyes and black hair. Can there be anything prettier than that? She said that she was a student at the school of natural sciences. First she came in to buy shampoo, then she came again, and that time, we talked a little and she laughed. The third time she came, she was crying, and asked me to help her find her aunt's house. She had its address, but didn't know how to get there. She said that she had come from Cairo to spend the day with her uncle, but his wife mistreated her, and she wanted to stay with another aunt. She said that she would not leave for Cairo without calling me, and that she was going to write to me afterwards, but two months have passed and she has neither called nor written. I will go see her in Cairo."

"And that is why you have been so preoccupied?" Hassanayn asked, but Magid didn't reply. It was as if his mind were already somewhere else. After that he went to Cairo every week, and came back saying "I don't know if she is at Cairo or 'Ayn Shams University. She didn't say what year she was, and

I believe she said that she was studying at the school of natural science, but I may be wrong. I don't know." Then he traveled again and came back to say, "It is difficult to enter the campus because of the university police and security. The university is like a fortress. I stand at the gate asking the students if they are at the school of natural science. Cairo University has more than one gate. I'm scared." He continued to make frequent trips to Cairo, and our meetings became fewer and fewer. Then winter came, and they stopped altogether.

※

Al-Dakruri came into my office, and before he'd even greeted me, he said, "Isn't it about time you left this badly lit office?"

I looked at him standing between my desk and the door, then asked, "Al-Dakruri, you are the president of the workers' union, aren't you?"

He smiled, and seemed as surprised as a little kid. Then his pale face turned red and he said, "Are you making fun of me?"

"Not at all, but I wanted to ask you why you never wear your overalls. I know that you are an electrical technician. Right?"

He laughed and said, "You're right, but I have forgotten all about electricity. There are always problems between the workers and the administration to be worked out, as you know."

I smiled. He always said that I knew things that I didn't actually know.

"Why do you want me to leave this office?" I asked.

"This is the normal thing for anyone to do," he said.

"You've been working here for ten years. You deserve to get a promotion and have additional employees working under your supervision. But they may forget about you like this. Write me a complaint, and I will look into it for you." I laughed and offered him a cigarette. He said that he had quit smoking because it was bad for one's health, and because he was trying to save enough money to get married, having delayed it for too long already.

"The President's reception ceremonies are going to be huge this time," he said. "The newspapers say that the Camp David meeting will end the Arab–Israeli conflict forever. They will broadcast the signing of the treaty on air the day after tomorrow, so get ready."

"Am I going to take the workers to the rally? You know that I have stopped doing that."

"You will regain the workers' respect for you by doing it this time. It is true that a long time has passed since what happened, but it's necessary to fully regain their respect, and don't forget that the new chairman doesn't know anything about it. You have to take the workers to a rally at least one more time to erase all memory of the old incident among the workers and employees."

He went out and left me thinking about what he was doing. How could he know that I was a thief, and still show no objection or surprise about it? And why was he so concerned about me regaining respect one and a half years after the incident? Surely, that was enough time to erase all memory of the incident, which, in fact, didn't really concern anybody except me. He always wanted me to be promoted. This al-Dakruri must be a messenger of divine providence, a prophet maybe. I thought about what he had said about saving money for his marriage, felt sorry for him, and liked him even more. I also felt that I did indeed need to regain the workers' respect.

❈

The day before our scheduled trip to Cairo, I called Usta Zinhum, and he came to see me in my office. I told him that this time we were going to take five hundred workers and four drivers. He already knew about it. I asked him about the fourth driver, who was coming with us for the first time, and he said that he would take care of him. Then I explained to Usta Zinhum that he should come alone to meet me at five in the morning in the square outside Masr Station and should leave the bus parked in front of his house. I also told him to ask the three other drivers to come and meet me at Aqta' Café between six and seven, and leave their buses parked in front of their houses as well, or in any other place they chose so that no one from the shipyard could see them.

"Aren't we going to spend the day somewhere?" he asked.

"We'll finish this job before it even begins," I said, and he smiled, then asked me about the pre-prepared meals which would be loaded in the buses for the workers. I laughed and said, "Sell them and share the revenue with the other drivers, or eat them."

At five o'clock the next morning, I was standing at the station, wearing two pullovers, and still chilled with the cold of March. It was still dark. Usta Zinhum arrived, looking like a big round ball because of the pile of clothes that he had put on. He seemed to be rolling along the ground. I handed him four lists with the names of the workers, and asked him to cross off the name of each worker as he arrived to receive his pay. We must have stood out in the sleepy square, for the workers found us pretty quickly. Usta Zinhum crossed out the names as I handed each worker three pounds. At six-thirty, I met the three drivers at Aqta' Café. There was a little more movement in the square, which was lazily waking up around us.

"Mr. Shagara, we really like you, but life is difficult these days," said the driver who had objected to the hundred pounds last time, then taken them, and then offered to return them when the trick was discovered. "We want two hundred pounds each."

I looked at the fourth driver, who was going out with us for the first time, and who was engrossed in drinking a glass of tea with milk in complete silence, as if the whole matter didn't concern him. His silence stirred my fears—something about him suggested a hardened criminal.

"Is this a mutiny?" I asked.

"We'll make it up to you next time," said Usta Zinhum, looking at the ground. So it was he who planned it, this old man bundled up in his clothes like a ball. I had decided to give each driver a hundred pounds, and save six hundred, having taken two pounds from the pay of each of the five hundred workers.

"What if I refuse?"

"We won't ruin our friendship. We won't take anything at all," they said, almost together. So they would let the crime be all mine. My face must have shown signs of consent, for I saw Usta Zinhum smile, and heard the new driver say, "The President will always be there, the people will be there, and we have loads of problems with other nations, and there will be no end to the visitors and the treaties."

So the scoundrel has finally said something! He was quite firm, and soon went back to sipping his tea. So be it.

I smiled and said, "It seems that this will be the last time."

When I returned to the apartment, I remembered the five hundred meals which Zinhum must have sold or even left at the store and received a cash refund. I was quite mad at first, and then I laughed at it all.

❄

It had been a month since I had last visited my parents' graves. I left work at eleven o'clock in the morning, and went to Masr Bank to deposit the new two hundred pounds in my account. I walked a little down Salah Salim Street, and in Manshiyya I found myself getting on the number five tram. What made me do that? It must have been my parents. I had thought of visiting them before, but I had never gotten around to it. My desire must have been stronger this time. It was one-thirty in the afternoon, and it was not yet summer, but the tram was crowded. I picked a spot next to the conductor, who was sitting by the back door. I leaned against the side of the tram. I was too preoccupied to let the crowding bother me. I didn't want to complain to my parents about anything. I didn't want to apologize for anything. I wanted only to see them, even in a dream. I didn't have any photographs of either of them, and I had nearly forgotten what they looked like.

Suddenly I felt someone looking at me. I looked around and found a woman with a brilliant smile watching me. I was confused. I wasn't ready for any adventures, so I tried to fix my eyes on my feet, but I continued to feel her gentle gaze on my face. I could not help looking up at her. She looked both radiant and a bit surprised. Her face disappeared behind a tall man who stood between us. It was over, but I kept trying to get another peek at her face every time the tall man moved. I didn't realize that my attempts were embarrassing him, until I caught his eyes and saw that he was both uncomfortable and suspicious. I lowered my eyes and calmed myself.

At the entrance of the cemetery, I was received by dirty barefoot children begging for "charity," skinny Quran reciters who hopped like wagtails and recited too quickly Quranic verses they didn't know very well. I almost left. I needed to cry. I knew that, but I didn't know why. I needed the tears to wash my soul, to clear my heart and mind of their burdens. Have I really turned out the way my father asked God that I would? At my parents' graves, I stood alone, having waved my arms and shooed the kids and the reciters away. I suddenly remembered who the woman who had smiled at me on the tram was. She was Kawthar, Hani's sister, who had been also like a sister to me in beautiful times past.

❀

A month later, I was in a taxi, and couldn't believe that the road the driver had taken was going to take us where I wanted to go. He was driving in alleys flanked by tall buildings that blocked the light and left the alleys quite dark, and streets that were crowded with workshops and cafés. He stopped in front of an area filled with shabby dark-colored tents, and said: "Here we are."

He was right. There was the hospital, with its bare trees standing farther apart from each other than I remembered. A few people were looking out of each of its windows, and the houses around it looked as if they were frightened by their gloomy surroundings.

"As you can see, I can't go any further," the driver said.

"What is this?"

"You must have been gone a while. Those are shelters."

I left the taxi and was met by clouds of moths and flies and a foul, stagnant stench. Should I go back? Why did I come, then? I stepped forward.

Naked children and pale women were standing outside the tents and tin shacks. A few men were busy with some wooden boards and tin sheets, and they all looked very desolate. Feces, feces! There were feces everywhere on the ground. A mesh of wires was hanging over the shelters, and I could hear the sounds of televisions and radios. There was only one meter between the tents and the entrance to the building across from them, and it was filled with chickens and ducks running in the mud and the bodies of dead cats. Where has God gone now? In the past, He had given us His paradise, so how could He leave us now? And in such a short time?

What a fool I am. A long time has passed. How had I failed to notice that when I brushed my hair in front of the mirror every morning? Oh Kawthar, did you have to look at me? I will probably not find anyone. You must have gotten married. A woman like you does not remain unmarried for long. Your amazing beauty and sweet fragrance stir the heart. Your face has become fuller and rounder, the face of a mature woman. I will not find you or Hani, who must be living with his wife in Cairo. Didn't he tell me when I ran into him at Raml Station that he was going to call his fiancée in Cairo? Here I'm at the entrance of the dark stairway, where a man with a swollen face lies with his crutch next to his one leg. He doesn't notice me going in as I tiptoe past him. He's surrounded by chickens and ducks. The windows on the stairway are all closed and covered with dust and cobwebs. It's pitch dark. Here I'm going up the stairs in the dark without meeting a single person, not a young man whom I knew as a child or an old man who might ask me about my parents. I know that a law was passed just after we left our apartment here, giving the residents permanent ownership of their apartments. Maybe this law was among the causes of my father's death soon after our move, for he saw it as the ultimate proof of bad luck. Maybe he neither disliked the hills nor wished to disappoint me. Yet, it is impossible to live here, even after that law. No one can live in a place that God has deserted.

But I'm going up the stairs. I will not miss your apartment, Kawthar. It was larger than ours. Your father had finished grade school, and so got a three-bedroom apartment when he was employed. Will Ahlam meet me? Your little sister whom I remembered on the day you smiled at me in the tram. She had passed her grade-school exams on the day we moved out of here. She must be a grown woman now, and it is for her that I'm here today.

Ahlam had your fragrance when you and I were growing up together. You always matured faster than I did, while she remained a child to me. Maybe if she sees me, she will remember how I used to make her feel better after Hani, who was always joking, had teased her and then asked her to make us some mint tea. She would leave the room angrily, and a little later you would bring in the tea with a smile and rosy cheeks, and you would also offer us peanuts and pumpkin seeds. Sometimes you told us that a good movie was showing that evening on the new television set your father had just bought, and sometimes you said how relieved you were that you had quit after middle school, and didn't have to study anymore, and sometimes you complained that nothing was on television except Gamal 'Abd al-Nassir receiving other Arab presidents and kings all day. Do you remember that I tried to explain to you that the Arab leaders were coming for a summit meeting, and you shrugged and said: "What summit?" Hani and I both laughed at your response, and Hani said that his family was a bunch of losers.

The door is now open and I do not see Ahlam. Who is this little dark girl standing in the door?

"Who is it, Nur?" called a voice from inside. It sounded like Kawthar's voice, with its distinctive hoarseness, which I can always recognize. So this little girl looking up at me was named Nur. What a distance there was between my eyes and hers.

"Who are you?" she asked quite casually. I smiled at her, but didn't reply. She ran inside, and I heard her say, "Mom, it is a very tall man who doesn't talk at all!"

I didn't hear footsteps, but I saw Kawthar in front of me with her feet bare. Her blonde hair fell loosely down her back, but she no longer had her sweet fragrance.

"Shagara! I mean, Mr. Shagara, please come in."

8

There is always a huge crowd on al-Tarikh Bridge every Wednesday. Young and old men and children in rags and bare feet start to arrive in the early morning and line up on the bridge with their faces toward the port, their gazes fixed on the empty space. The tram stops at its station behind them, and no one leaves his spot until evening.

A long time after this started happening, the people realized that there was an incinerator at the port where the police burned drugs they had confiscated after stopping smuggling attempts or raiding dealers' storage places. Wednesday was the day on which the burning took place, and the sea breeze blowing at the bridge always passed the incinerator and, carrying the smoke of burning hashish, brought the people on the bridge pleasure and comfort free of charge. Now many vehicles besides the tram loiter on the bridge on Wednesdays.

I was sitting in my office thinking of how women lived longer than men because God wanted them to suffer longer. Why did

God want His beautiful creatures to suffer? I felt that my mind was about to burst, and I was scared. . .

Kawthar's mother had cried when she saw me. Her husband, 'Abd al-'Al, had died of sorrow for Hani, who was killed in Sinai during the war. Mr. 'Abd al-'Al was a distinguished person in the neighborhood. He was a handsome man who had passed his good looks down to his daughters. He was always clean and nicely dressed, and wore a full suit in both winter and summer. He was a quiet man who talked very little. He often came into the room where Hani and I used to study in the evenings, opened a small closet with a key that he kept, took out a small book and left. Hani used to talk to me about his father's wide knowledge of poets and poetry.

Nur, Kawthar's little girl, was dark because her father, who left her and two other children and went to work in Dubai, was dark. Where is this Dubai on the world map? And how can I get to it now? Ahlam had quietly married a month ago and left for Dubai with her husband as well. Maybe Ahlam was married on the same day on which I saw Kawthar in the tram.

Why did I not expect all this? Why did I forget that there had been a big war in October 1973, and that many people had been killed in this war? Was it because 'Abd al-Salam, who was besieged with the third army, had returned safely? Was 'Abd al-Salam our entire army?

Why did I not realize that as Ahlam grew up she also matured and came to have her own magic and secret world? As soon as I had entered the apartment, I had a sudden cold impression that I didn't really know anyone there, and that feeling didn't surprise me. If you lose something and then find it again when you don't need it anymore, does it mean anything? Kawthar must have felt the same way. She sat down and smiled, then got up and brought her mother, leaning on her arm, to sit with us. We sat in silence, and all the mother said was: "How are you, son?" Then she started to weep quietly. Kawthar helped her up, and took her out of the room, then came back to say that her mother never stopped crying. So it was not seeing me that made her cry as I had thought. It was not that I reminded her of her son, his childhood and early youth. I didn't feel like talking to Kawthar about anything, and she didn't ask me about my parents. I don't think that she even wondered about the cause of my strange visit. When we had been silent for too long, I started to ask questions, and the answers were like blows on my head. Did Kawthar think that I knew every misfortune that happened to them? I didn't ask her about Rashid. If Hani, who never stopped joking and laughing, was dead, then Rashid, who used to memorize and sing 'Abd al-Halim's songs, must have been suffering in the "Loyalty and Hope" institution for the disabled. Is life a tasteless farce or a futile tragedy? I wasn't surprised that Kawthar had smiled at me in the tram. She must have remembered that this tall man in front of her was once her neighbor, and maybe she remembered that I had kissed her once, and she thought of her husband and enjoyed a pleasant moment. She probably didn't expect anything more than a smile in return.

❋

I was struck by a frenzy of desire, so I went around our shipyard offices peeking at the legs of the female employees. I sat with the ones I knew and chatted in order to get a look at the breasts tucked inside their clothes and smell their cheap and heavy perfumes. I imagined them in sexual positions with their husbands, whom I either knew if they worked in our shipyard or didn't know. At home, I created an imaginary palace of sexual pleasures and got so good at my fantasizing that I could ejaculate without touching myself.

When al-Dakruri came to visit me, he was horrified to see my long beard and my bushy unbrushed hair, which had not been washed in a long time.

"Shagara, you should get married," he said. A sarcastic smile came to my face.

"You have an apartment, so what are you waiting for? You are in a better position than I am."

I did not reply.

"Money? It's on its way. Prepare yourself. Begin has arrived in Alexandria, as you know, and the day after tomorrow he will leave Ras al-Tin Palace to go to the President's summer house in Ma'mura. The shipyard will participate in greeting them on Gamal 'Abd al-Nassir Street.

Screw him! I almost screamed at al-Dakruri, almost picked him up and threw him out the window into the back street. He knew everything about me and didn't object or ask for anything in return for his silence. What kind of a person was he? He was not a saint, an angel, or a devil. He didn't deserve to be thanked or cursed. And who was I, exactly? I didn't even know that Begin had arrived in Alexandria. I no longer read any newspapers or watched television news programs. I was on a quest for women, women's scents, sweat, lips, breasts, and I was thinking of buying a color television set in order to look at their warm flesh. This Begin was the one who had thrown God out of His land where the government housing in Kum al-Shuqafa stood, and he was the one who filled the area with a shanty town.

86

I'm not an idiot, as you all must think. I understand how things work. I really do. I only have one modest desire—I want to find a woman to marry. Then I would become even more isolated, my life would revolve around her and our children, and I would become even more stupid. This is the desire which has never been fulfilled, and which I have always tried to ignore. I'm Shagara Muhammad 'Ali, the tall dark man with the attractive face and the black eyes, strong as a wall, manhood running thick in my veins, almost bursting out of my skin, turning my blood into fire, and pouring out effortlessly. I have an apartment and more than five hundred pounds in my bank account. I have no relatives, and both my parents are dead. I, Shagara Muhammad 'Ali, cannot find a woman. Isn't there one single girl courageous enough to come forward and end my loneliness? Isn't there one of my colleagues who could present a friend or a sister that I could marry? Why have women given up their historical role of trying to secure a man for themselves? And they want me to participate in Begin's reception? Shit! I will receive Begin and Begin's mother! I will make the employees like him. I won't steal any of their pay this time. I will sit at the café near the train station, and leave them in the street, in the square in front of the station, where the buildings are far apart and the sunlight scorches the ground without a single spot of shade. I will carry out this dirty mission to the end.

⁂

The door bell rang, and I opened it to find Hassanayn standing there with his arms open and his face as flushed as ever. I was very happy to see him.

"I received my B.A.," he said. It was the first time that any of my friends had visited me at home since my mother's death. We hugged, and I wasn't sure whether I was hugging him because he had received his degree or because he was visiting me.

"I'm happy for you and for myself," I said. "For your graduation and for your visit." We were standing in the empty hallway, so I led him to the balcony, where there was an old chair, and I brought another chair for myself.

"It's true that we haven't been very good to you," he said with real sorrow in his voice.

"Don't worry about it," I said. "Congratulations on your B.A." He was looking at my thick beard, the dark circles of exhaustion around my eyes and the swelling beneath them, which was due to insomnia and excessive smoking.

"I will shave for your sake," I said. Then I went to the bathroom, shaved, and returned to find him with a big smile on his red face. He must have been wondering at the way I behaved.

"Between you and me, I think it's worthless," he said.

"What is?"

"The B.A." We both laughed, then he went on: "I'm thirty-six, and my salary now is higher than that of any new university graduate. The important thing is that I'm through with wars and conspiracies, with studying history."

We laughed for a few moments. He seemed to be refreshed by the view of the sea before us. I asked him if he wanted something to drink, and he said no. Then he asked if we could go to the café.

"I went to the café more than once, and didn't find any of you there," he said.

"Why didn't you go see Magid at the pharmacy or come here?"

He looked as if he were at a loss at how to answer, and he blushed, then said, "I don't know."

We got up to go to the café, and I said, "We no longer function according to the same secret clock."

But shortly after we arrived at the café, we saw Magid coming. Hassanayn looked as happy as a small child, and he cried, "Here we are again, getting together without any plans." Hassanayn seemed to be truly overjoyed, nothing like the person 'Abd al-Salam had once described as permanently contented, enjoying the bliss of contentment and avoiding all of the more powerful emotions.

"Many people like to stick to smooth roads, even if they don't lead anywhere," 'Abd al-Salam had once said. "The important thing isn't where they lead, but that they are smooth. Maybe it's also a matter of age, because after thirty the level of ambition decreases and people's lives fall into a pattern, which they only break if they go insane."

"Hassanayn has received his B.A.," I told Magid after we hugged.

"Congratulations. Now you will start making real history!" Magid said with a wide smile. Then he laughed and added, "Don't you dare ask me about Cairo and the school of natural science!"

Hassanayn and I looked at each other. Magid had just reminded us of a long-forgotten matter. We both cried at once, "So you found her?"

"Of course I did."

"Boy! I bet she couldn't believe all the trouble you went through," I said.

"Of course she didn't," Magid said, then turned to the waiter and said, "Bring us a backgammon board, Muhsin."

"Wait a minute," I said. "First tell us how you found her, and what happened." Magid took off his glasses, started wiping them, then said without looking up at us: "I never found her. I was just joking. The whole thing was crazy, anyway. Now I'm studying German at the Goethe Institute. I'll be traveling to Austria."

❋

Magid told us that he had bought a used Fiat and was planning to drive us around the city at night. He also said that Dr. Musa, who worked in the pharmacy with him, had secured a job for himself in Kuwait, and that he was now satisfied, was working hard, and treating the customers nicely.

I told them about something that had happened in my building recently. Two weeks earlier, I had heard a noise on the stairs. I was excited at the thought of another resident moving in. I hadn't seen a single resident in the building from the summer of 1976 until the summer of this year, 1979. I didn't know what all the tenants were doing abroad for so long. For three whole years, I had locked the entrance to the building every night. . . I opened the door and, as I expected, saw delivery men carrying new furniture. I stood on the stairs for a moment listening to the sound of footsteps coming up and the carefree laughs of a young couple, who soon came up to where I was. There was an older woman who looked like she could be the girl's mother. I was embarrassed at my intrusion and ashamed of my shaggy beard, but I remained standing on the stairs outside my apartment.

"Do you live here?" the young man, who had very thick hair, asked me.

"Yes."

"Then you must be Mr. Shagara," said the girl with a smile as she looked up at me. I realized that 'Abdu al-Fakahani must have told them about me and given them a key to the front door. I also realized that it must have been 'Abdu who gave the police a key on the night when they came to arrest me. Maybe that was why he had seemed to be afraid of me when I went to see him after I was released, and maybe he thought that I was really dangerous. But that was an old story, and I should not have bothered with it anymore. Besides, the police would have gotten in with or without the key.

"Yes," I finally answered.

"Do you live alone, son?" asked the mother.

"Yes."

"Then you will let us enjoy your company," they all said at once, and then laughed. I smiled, but felt myself blush. I also felt that they were a bunch of barbarians. I'm not sure how I felt about them exactly. . . I was almost dancing with joy in my apartment for the rest of the day, for no matter what they were, they were still people who were going to live with me in this huge building. Besides, I saw the girl's face become a bit pale after they all laughed. It was Friday, and I was getting ready to go fishing. I had bought some fishing equipment but I had not used it yet. I didn't even use it that day, but never mind. I will use it some day. I took off my clothes and put on my bathing suit, but then I didn't actually leave. I kept going out to the balcony and listening to the sounds of moving furniture on the floor above. I kept looking up, and one of them was always looking out from the balcony above mine. I was embarrassed every time our eyes met, but the other person always smiled and waved at me. I thought that I was going crazy, and that they were too. They should have at least found my nakedness distasteful, especially because their balcony was about half a meter smaller than mine and allowed them to see me fully.

I thought that maybe they were truly happy to discover they had a neighbor, but I wondered why I was so excited. Residents moving into one of the apartments in the building could not explain such excitement. It was all quite silly, and I was annoyed at my foolishness. In the evening I went to see Magid at the pharmacy, but he wasn't there. I bought a cream to relieve rheumatic pains from Dr. Musa. I was starting to have rheumatic pains because I slept naked at night and the apartment was empty. I once heard my father say that furniture breathes in a place and makes it warmer—but a woman would have been even better. She would breathe warmth like a steam engine. I know this is true, even though I haven't tried it. I was afraid that I was bound to live alone until I died, and I even thought of asking 'Abdu al-Fakahani to find me a wife—yes, ask him to sell me a woman and buy me in exchange!

Magid and Hassanayn laughed heartily at my story, which I told without many of the details that I just wrote, and I almost wished that I hadn't said the last sentence. Magid said that 'Abdu al-Fakahani doesn't care for such minor exchanges, that he was now trading in big plots of land in 'Agami, and that he had recently bought five feddans on Abu Yusif beach and another five on Abu Talat beach.

Magid had learned all this from some of his customers at the pharmacy, who used to be Bedouins and were now driving Peugeots and Jeeps. He said that they had sold the lands which their parents had traditionally planted with figs to tourism companies or to individual investors, often Egyptians who had been working in one of the Gulf countries. Magid also said that they were often surprised to know that he didn't sell aphrodisiacs at his pharmacy and didn't know how to prepare them.

"There will come a day when we won't be able to find a single fig. What a tragedy!" Hassanayn said gravely, and we all laughed. Then he turned to me and asked, "Are you really thinking of marriage?"

"Of course I am."

"Then finish your story, and we will find you a wife," he said, and went on laughing. I wasn't upset. I felt that it was just an innocent joke, and I went on with the story.

I told them how I had been unable to sleep the previous night. I watched television until the end of the broadcast, and was thinking of a strange dance that appeared on the show "We Chose It for You." The dance ended with the hands of the male dancers placed on the rear ends of the female dancers. It was quite a scene! It almost jumped out of the television screen at my face. How is it that television shows are so daring these days? Anyway, that wasn't all that happened that night.

A little before dawn, I heard a loud splash in the sea. I heard the sound repeatedly and thought that a ship might have drifted to the shore, but then I realized that this was impossible because the ship would get stuck in the sand long before it reached the shore. I opened the window and cold air struck my face. I saw several dark objects floating on the surface of the waves. I turned on the balcony light and stood there. Chairs, mattresses, boards, suitcases, and many other pieces of furniture were flying off the balcony above mine. Each item glowed briefly in the light of my balcony before sinking into the darkness below and finally splashing into the sea. It was the same furniture that I had seen the delivery men bring up two weeks earlier. Of course I didn't hesitate to go up to the apartment above. I wasn't scared, and didn't find the matter surprising for long. I was sure that it was the work of an intruder in my neighbors' apartment. I expected a fight, so I took a knife with me.

When I got to the door of their apartment, I found it open, so I tiptoed inside. I saw the young man whom I had seen earlier with the girl and her mother. He was wearing only a bathing suit, and his thick hair was sticking out like the quills of a porcupine.

"Can I help you?" he growled at me with a fierce look.

"I'm sorry," I mumbled as I retreated out of his apartment.

"What do you say we all spend the rest of the night in Qabbari?" Hassanayn suggested. "Hagg Luqman has set up a big tent for his election campaign that's worth seeing."

It was almost ten o'clock, and the effect of my story on my two friends was gone except for occasional smiles that appeared on their lips every now and then when they interrupted the backgammon game and looked at me. We had exhausted all the comments and jokes that we could make about the story, all revolving around how strangely people behaved these days. We laughed hardest when Hassanayn said, "If he had decided to get rid of his furniture, why didn't he give it to you or ask you if you knew someone who needed it?"

Magid was not in favor of going to Qabbari because he wanted to drive us around the city as he had promised. He pointed to the steady flow of cars coming from 'Agami and said, "We should spend the night in Bahari like other car owners."

As usual, I was uninterested in the elections. I knew that President Sadat had dissolved the People's Assembly, and that there were going to be elections for the new members. I also knew that there was strong popular opposition to the Camp David agreement and that the government newspapers were fiercely attacking the opposition parties, but I never really bothered to read the details or get into any conversations about what was going on. I saw several signs hanging on stores and on the streets with pledges of support for Hagg Luqman, but I didn't care. I don't remember ever having voted in any elections or referenda. I don't even carry a voter's registration card, although I still keep my father's card with all the other papers of his that I have kept since he died.

Besides, I had completely stopped committing my crimes, because the President still flew to Alexandria in his helicopter on the twenty-sixth of July and his visitors from among the other world leaders came only in the winter, when he was usually in Aswan. I sometimes thought that they came to enjoy the warm Aswan sun and take the opportunity to be cured of rheumatism rather than to meet with the President. The ship-yard still sent a few members of the workers' union to participate in the Labor Day ceremony. When I was told to lead the workers who were sent to take part in Begin's reception, I did exactly as I was told, and didn't make a single penny off of the assignment.

"Who is Hagg Luqman?" I asked, without any real interest.

"There isn't a single person in Alexandria who doesn't know who Hagg Luqman is," Magid said. "Even I have had the honor of meeting him. One day a black Mercedes stopped in front of the pharmacy, and the driver came in to buy five boxes of Givrin. I saw Hagg Luqman in the back seat and he waved at me. I recognized him from the pictures that were hanging everywhere, and I waved back. Then I saw him get out of the car, and thought that he was going to come into the pharmacy to talk to me about the upcoming elections, but he only walked into the side alley, then walked out, buttoning his pants, and got back into his car."

We all laughed. Hassanayn was surprised at the large amount of Givrin which Hagg Luqman had bought. I wondered if he were really ill, but Magid said that Givrin was a general dietary supplement and also effective as an aphrodisiac.

"You only saw him once," Hassanayn said to Magid, "but I have seen him many times. At the Lansh Café in Mafruza he used to sell goods stolen from the customs warehouse, such as sweaters, jeans, and transistor radios. Then he disappeared about three ago, and when he returned he had acquired the title Hagg and was known to be one of the biggest importers of girders in Egypt. He's worth seeing, especially since I've heard that he gives public speeches even though he's illiterate. Come on! We have nothing to lose. If we don't like it, we can still go to Bahari."

❋

We got into Magid's car and for the whole trip I was thinking about what a crazy mood we were in. This whole trip was a joke and we took it no more seriously than a game of backgammon. When we got to Qabbari, I almost asked Magid to drive on to Bahari, but I saw the white and yellow lights on Sidi al-Qabbari Street making the night as bright as the middle of the day. There was a huge crowd of people and a tent which took up half the street, and I became really curious to see this Hagg Luqman who could attract so many people.

Magid had a hard time finding a place to park on one of the nearby side streets. We had to push our way through the huge crowd to get to the entrance of the tent. It was only by chance that I was ahead of Magid and Hassanayn when we walked in.

"The men of Dikhayla have arrived," a man shouted, raising both his arms high in the air to point at us and at the stage where Hagg Luqman was seated in the midst of a large number of men in dark suits and *galabiyyas*. Hagg Luqman was wearing a dark glittery suit. His dark face glittered as well and looked as if it had been rubbed with oil. "The men of Dikhayla have arrived," the man yelled out again, and I recognized him as al-Dakruri, the head of the workers' union at the shipyard. I was surprised to see him here, and wondered what he was doing and what his relationship to Hagg Luqman was.

The men on the stage craned their necks to look at us, and Hagg Luqman greeted us with a slight nod of his big head, while al-Dakruri made room for us to be seated in the front row. We put on a grave look, appropriate for the "men of Dikhayla," as he had called us. I heard Magid say that we would never be able to walk out of this trap. Shortly after we sat down, al-Dakruri approached us and grabbed me by the arm. He wanted me to follow him, so I did, and it struck me that I looked like a blind man being led by the arm. We stopped behind the stage and he said, "Wait here and don't move."

I stood there on ground which had been covered with sand, paying no attention to what he was up to. I was trying to read some of the calligraphy printed on the sides of the tent when he returned, carrying a small bulging envelope.

"The Hagg offers this envelope to you, and you will be responsible for the votes of the people of Dikhayla," al-Dakruri said. "I know you can do it."

Have I become a machine whose hand automatically stretches out to snatch up money? Hadn't I proved my honesty on the day of Begin's visit? I almost laughed, thinking that maybe al-Dakruri knew me better than I knew myself.

"Five hundred pounds," he said.

"Don't worry. He will win and all the competing candidates will fail," I said, after a few moments of silence. I was wondering whether I should share the money with Magid and Hassanayn or whether I should even tell them about it, but I boldly said, "This is a small sum for a neighborhood such as Dikhayla."

Al-Dakruri's eyes gleamed like those of a fox.

"Then we can just give it back," he said. I was flustered, even though I was capable of sending him flying in the air with a single blow.

"Give my congratulations to the Hagg. The votes of Dikhayla will all be for him," I said. Then I took the money out of the envelope and stuffed it in my pocket. I was walking away from him when he stopped me and whispered in my ear: "The Hagg will give me an apartment."

※

I found myself walking toward the street which I had been avoiding for some time. I saw that the house of jasmine was completely dark. No sweet scent met my nose anymore. The flowers were wilted, and the leaves on the trees were dry and dusty and many of them had fallen to the street, where they crackled under my feet. I saw a huge lock on the gate. Under the light of the sole street lamp, which was in front of 'Abd al-Salam's house, I looked at the pipes on the walls of the house of jasmine, where the paint was peeling and moisture had left several large stains, and I saw a ferret climbing upward.

9

A man and a woman got married, and the next morning several members of the bride's family went to visit them. When no one opened the door, they broke it down and found the man on top of his bride, unable to pull his animal out of her. They were both in tears, having tried in vain all night to separate themselves. The relatives wrapped the couple in a sheet and took them to a hospital, where they were separated and returned to their apartment by midnight.

Two days later, the same thing happened again, and the man cried for help from the neighbors, who carried them to the hospital, wrapped in the sheet. They returned, separated, shortly after midnight.

People started whispering, pointing up at the high apartment and laughing every time they passed the building. Then a month passed and nothing more happened. No one knew that the couple had lost their ability to have intercourse.

But finally they went back to it, and then tore the flesh off of their own faces with their fingernails out of fear and repentance for what they had done. The man had to cry for the *neighbors' help once again, and they took the couple to the hospital to be separated, and the couple returned home at dawn. In the morning the man stood alone on the fifth-floor balcony, screaming and slapping his face. He was looking at the street below as if he were going to jump off the balcony. His bride came out and threw herself to the street. He watched her body hit the pavement and make one movement, like a final throb.*

I opened the door to the balcony and walked out. I was wrapped in the bright daylight that extended infinitely in front of me and felt as if I were flying in space. I looked down and saw the sea as an azure velvet carpet, and I could almost feel its softness as I stood barefoot on the balcony's tiled floor. I looked up and saw the dome of the sky, so close. Its pure blue tempted me to jump up and touch it with my hands. This was a day unlike any other that I could remember. Perhaps God had returned to live with us as He had when we were children.

I took my fishing rod, my basket, line and hooks, and went to the beach. I hadn't planned on going fishing, and hadn't bought any bait, but I figured that I would find someone to sell me some on the beach. This was a day on which nothing could go wrong.

As soon as I closed my door and turned to walk down the stairs, I saw a pretty child going up. He was having trouble climbing the stairs and had placed his hands on his knees and was pressing on them with every step he climbed. He was wearing a white *galabiyya* and his surprise at seeing me showed in his bright black eyes, so I smiled at him. Before I had a chance to ask him what he wanted and why he had come into the building, I heard a woman calling him from one of the floors above.

"Hurry, Ziyad," she said.

"All right," he replied, and sighed, looking at me with a smile as if he were asking me to witness his exhaustion and the height of the stairs. So one of the apartments must be occupied, and this beautiful child only went down this morning so that I could see him on his way back and add to my joys of the day. But when had these residents moved into their apartment? When had they moved their furniture? How had I failed to notice them? I found that I was galloping down the stairs like a horse.

In the evening, the weather changed, and when it became cold I realized that fall was coming to an end. We were nearing the rainy days, when the rain would be so heavy that you would think it was unaware of the presence of people on earth.

"You have obviously become a skillful fisherman," said Magid when I went to the pharmacy to give him part of the catch. We were sitting at a small desk in a corner of the pharmacy.

"I'm thinking of buying another fishing kit," I said, and it was true. The area behind the airport was rocky and deep and had plenty of fish on warm and hot days. I was always relieved by fishing—fighting with the fish and wishing I could catch the heart of the sea. Fishing to me was not just a hobby or an amusement, but nor did I need the fish, since I wasn't supporting a family who might need to eat them. To me fishing was a fight, but that day I didn't feel the same power that I had felt in the past.

"I'm sorry that I can't come to the café these days," Magid said. "Dr. Musa has gone to Kuwait, and there is no one to help me here."

"I haven't been going there myself," I said, then added with a wide smile, "I saw some new residents this morning."

"Really? How wonderful. You are a hero to have stayed alone in the building for so long. I only hope that they don't throw their furniture into the sea."

We were both laughing when a woman walked into the pharmacy. She was wearing a cheap dress and carrying a child who could not stop coughing, trembling as he did so. She was holding him tightly in her arms to keep him from falling. Magid got up and stood behind the counter. She could not raise her hand to give him the prescription, so he leaned forward and took it from her. Then he went to the shelves where he kept the medicines and brought her what she needed. I was looking at the child's face, which I could see over his mother's shoulder—a tiny pale face with the tongue hanging out. Then I heard her say: "Here are two pounds." I saw Magid shake his head and smile. He reached out and patted the child on the head, then he put the medicines in a bag and leaned over the counter again to hang the bag on the woman's fingers. She turned toward me with an embarrassed smile, then hurried out.

"Wait!" Magid called out to her. She stopped at the door, and turned towards him.

"Yes," she said.

"Maybe you should take him to Shatbi Hospital."

"All right," she said, then disappeared into the street. He returned to his seat and sat in silence for a few minutes before he said, "She doesn't have enough money for the required medication, and the doctor has prescribed her enough medicine to kill a horse."

So he refused to take the two pounds from her, because it seemed that this was all the money she had. I thought of the five hundred pounds, about which I never said anything to him or to Hassanayn, and felt like leaving the place immediately, but I stayed and asked him, "Have you heard from Hassanayn lately? Does he come by sometimes?"

My questions set Magid giggling for a few minutes before he finally replied, "He came by a week ago for some prescriptions. I gave them to him as a gift together with a few bottles of perfume. He's gotten married."

"Married?"

"Yes. And I'd like to visit him, but I can't find the time."

"But he never said anything."

"He himself didn't know it was going to happen. He found himself all alone with his mother after the last of his sisters was married, so he decided to get married as well."

"And the apartment?"

"He's living in his mother's apartment."

Magid got up to help a few customers who had walked into the pharmacy, and left me thinking about all of the stupid questions which had come out of my mouth. So Hassanayn had solved the problem in the quickest way possible. Though why should I call it a problem? I noticed a copy of *Al-Ahram* on the desk. The headlines were about the explosions in Iran and the upcoming return of Khomeini to Tehran. Magid returned to his seat, but it was only a minute before a young man in jeans and a leather jacket came in. He smiled at us, but looked rather uncomfortable. Magid went up to him, and the man leaned toward him and whispered something in his ear.

"Sorry. I don't sell any of those," Magid said. The man left with his eyes fixed on the ground.

"He was asking about psychedelic drugs," Magid said with a shrug of his shoulders. I was surprised because the man didn't look like the kind of person who used these drugs.

Magid said that it was not a matter of looks, and that maybe he was just going to try them on the recommendation of one of his friends.

I remembered what 'Abd al-Salam had said about Magid—that he still had a baby face, which hadn't changed since they were in high school. The years didn't leave their mark on Magid's face. His hair was still as black and soft as it had always been, and he always had a big smile. We sometimes thought that if Magid walked through a sand storm, he would come out of it without a speck of dust on him. He always reminded you of a child whose mother had just cleaned and groomed him before letting him out.

"Are you making progress in German?" I asked him.

"I have quit studying German," he answered. "I met an American woman who said that she would help me travel to the United States. I ran into her in a pharmacy in 'Agami. She said that I shouldn't be studying German when my English is so good, that it would be better to improve on what I already know than to start all over again with something new. She also said that she would be willing to help me join an American institute or one of the pharmaceutical companies. She's in Cairo now. She came to Egypt with her husband, who is an investor in some projects here, and they will both leave next January. She sent me a letter from Cairo to confirm what she had told me."

He was talking seriously and with a lot of confidence, and I wondered why he wanted to travel. I was touring the glass medicine cabinets with my eyes and wondering if there were really as many diseases in the world as all these different medicines, how many sick people there were, and if anyone was actually healthy. Or were we all living with germs and microbes which were always waiting for their chance to attack?

The gates of heaven opened and poured down their inevitable supply of rain. Alexandria curled up like a ball, and the days became extensions of the nights. I forgot about Hassanayn and my plans to visit him. When I left my house at six o'clock every morning, it was like going out at midnight. I walked close to the walls, trying to avoid the mud on the streets and the water pouring out of the drain pipes. I supported myself with my hand against the walls, walked so close to them that my face and chest almost touched them, and yet I nearly slipped more than once. I saw the people around me doing the same thing and it struck me that we all resembled insects.

I didn't stop going to work. What would I do in an apartment with no electricity? I only had a few candles to light up the place. There was very little work to do, and many employees were delayed by the rains. The newspapers I read in my office said that the stormy winter had caused the port to close down, and that the ships couldn't enter it to off-load. I wished that there were a famine. I wanted to see people eat their children after consuming all the cats and dogs in the city!

The newspapers also talked about changes in the atmosphere of the earth as a result of the nuclear experiments that were carried out openly by the powerful nations and discreetly by the smaller ones. Some scientists predicted the return of the ice age and the end of modern civilization. The television showed footage of rains in Europe, of streets and houses covered in snow, of train crashes and people freezing to death.

The employees in the shipyard said that it was the wrath of God on a nation where the men had become thieves and the women went around naked, but an employee who had just returned from Libya said that it was all because of Qaddafi, who was making the clouds rain out of season. He said that he himself had seen the airplanes fly up into the clouds and emit a chemical that dissolved the clouds over the cultivated areas of the desert. Furthermore, he added, the airplanes sometimes flew in search of clouds, which they drove in front of them like sheep to the areas that needed water, where the clouds were then dissolved into rain. He said that this process was depleting the clouds over North Africa, causing angry clouds from neighboring regions to fill the resulting vacuum. And what region is closer than Europe? He finished his story by saying that the world constantly maintains equilibrium—when a man dies in Japan, another is born in the United States.

He went from one office to another repeating his theory to the employees, and spent most of the day in the cafeteria, where the employees preferred to spend the cold days drinking hot tea. He was serious about his theory, and when the other employees laughed at him, he sought evidence and proof. He said that any high-school student knew that an area of low atmospheric pressure attracts wind, which can make the region cold or warm.

"God created the world at an equilibrium which Man alone has disturbed, and the High Dam is a prime example of that," he added. "The dam has caused the erosion of the Egyptian coast on the Mediterranean, giving the sea the upper hand over the land. In the past, the Nile unloaded its silt into the sea, reducing the strength of the waves and the salinity of the seawater, preventing erosion. Now the sea freely beats against the coast and in less than five years, both Damietta and Rosetta will disappear from the map. The same problem will face the Nile Valley, which itself is the sedimentation of silt over millions of years. The silt came with the floods every year to counter the effects of the sand that came with the winds from the east and the west. Now the agricultural lands of the valley are being eroded, invaded by sand, and with no silt to counter its effects, it will be less than a hundred years before the Nile Valley disappears and Egypt becomes all desert again. Nature has been kind to us, but we are bastards."

At times I thought he was right, and I was afraid. Then I asked myself what I had to fear. I didn't care about Damietta because I wasn't going to buy any furniture from there. I didn't care about Rosetta either, since I caught my own fish behind the airport. And I didn't care what happened to the whole country in a hundred years, because I wasn't going to live that long, unless God challenged me, and I didn't think that he would do that to an orphan like me.

I returned to my apartment in the afternoon and felt as though it were midnight. Shivering with the cold, I took off my wet clothes, and found that the electricity was still out. I lit a few candles and sat in front of the silent television set, staring dismally into the air. I could hear the movements of children and the laughter of the new residents in the apartment on the upper floor. I thought that this might be another heroic deed to be added to my list—living alone among happy families. I remembered how my father once told me about a similar winter that drowned the village where he grew up. The houses dissolved under the torrents of rain, and the mud was knee-high. Fires broke out as if it were raining oil and gasoline. The mosque collapsed on top of those who sought refuge inside it, and not an hour passed in which there were no wails over a cow that had died or an old person who had frozen to death. My father said that our family was all saved because his grandfather, Shagara, locked them inside the house and said that whatever happened to them would be the predestined will of God.

I remained silent day and night, watching the empty looks on people's faces, and thinking that the winter was not going to end before bringing some ill fate.

❋

Only a few people attended the funeral—the members of the workers' union, ten or so workers, Hagg Luqman, and me, the only administrative employee of the shipyard who was there. Hagg Luqman sat next to me and I shrank uncomfortably in my seat. I had taken five hundred pounds of his money and hadn't done anything to earn it. He had won the elections. He had known that he would win, and I didn't know why he had squandered his money the way he had. He must have squandered quite a bit. If I received five hundred pounds for a small neighborhood like Dikhayla, then how much did the representatives of such neighborhoods as 'Amriyya, Wardiyan, Mafruza, and Basal Port get?

In the house we were received by a young man who looked very much like al-Dakruri. I learned that he was his brother. He sat with us in a small room, and his eyes were bloodshot. There was a shaykh who looked quite confused and kept gathering the wet tails of his outfit around his knees. He recited the Quran, his voice, his ears, and his hands all shaking. In the middle of the room was a marble-top table with a few candles stuck on it, since the electricity was still out. We could hear the rain falling outside, and some of the people whispered,

"God have mercy on your worshippers." Hagg Luqman appeared to me to be the most distressed.

"Al-Dakruri was a fine young man," he said.

"He liked you too, Hagg, but we can't object to the will of God," replied al-Dakruri's brother.

What made Hagg Luqman go to Um Zughaib, near 'Amriyya, to inspect the iron wares stored in the desert in this terrible rain? And why did al-Dakruri go with him? What kind of snake suddenly slithered out of its den and chose to bite al-Dakruri, of all the people accompanying Hagg Luqman, on the back of his hand? Hagg Luqman said that they were astounded to see al-Dakruri suddenly screaming and writhing on the ground, his right hand open and stiff and his left hand holding the wrist of the right. Then they saw the greenish yellow snake wriggle away slowly, unaware of, or indifferent to, what it had done. Hagg Luqman said that he immediately took al-Dakruri to 'Amriyya Hospital in his Mercedes, which he drove himself, but that al-Dakruri had died on the way, even though the trip was only ten minutes in the Mercedes. Hagg Luqman finished his story by saying that the more he thought about the incident and about the way the snake looked, the more he was convinced that the snake had been sent to carry out God's will.

"Otherwise, we would not have been blinded to it," he concluded, "and it would not have crawled away in such peace and calm afterwards."

When we left al-Dakruri's house, we were met by the cold wind slapping our faces, and had to jog and hop in the rain, in the mud and the darkness everywhere.

※

"I'm sorry, but the rain kept me from visiting you earlier," I said to Hassanayn when I visited him in March, more than a month after the rain had stopped.

"Same here," he said. "This was not normal rain. It was the wrath of God."

He was wearing a robe of red wool, and a woolen hat. He looked very healthy, and his face was as red as if he had been standing in front of a burning oven. He called out to his wife, Ibtihal, who then came into the room, preceded by a sweet fragrance.

"This is Shagara, about whom I have told you," he said to her before turning to me, "I talk about nobody other than you, Magid, and 'Abd al-Salam. Is there any news of 'Abd al-Salam?"

I had gotten up to shake hands with her, and she had a very pleasant smile as we shook hands. I was confused by his question, which came just as I was about to congratulate her, and wasn't sure whether I should answer or go on and congratulate his wife. Then I sat down and again said, "I'm really sorry, Hassanayn." I felt really guilty. He was rubbing his hands together, and again called out to his wife, who returned carrying a china plate with a gray floral pattern. She placed the plate, which was covered in peeled oranges, on a low marble-top table in front of us. Then she left the room. Only a few minutes later he called her again and she came in with a similar plate of tangerines, then left. He called her again, and this time she came in with a plate of bananas. I was quite taken by the whole thing. I kept saying that this wasn't necessary, and she only smiled while he insisted and then said, "Tea, Ibtihal, then coffee." He kept offering me the fruits and insisting that I eat. I was a little hesitant, but I gave in to his adamant hospitality, and I ate and ate. The fruit tasted different from any I had eaten before, and I wondered if the fruit grown in Egypt had actually become sweeter or if it was just the warm and friendly family atmosphere surrounding me.

I looked at the freshly painted walls and the simple inexpensive chairs. Everything in the room looked beautiful and well matched. I watched Hassanayn as he kept calling out to his wife with the delight of a small child. He received her with eyes full of joy, which followed her everywhere, as if Hassanayn were too happy to believe that she was real. I thought that he was acting as if he had created her himself, otherwise what was the reason for such rapture and pride?

"So. What do you think of marriage?"

I had expected him to repeat his earlier question about 'Abd al-Salam, which I had not had a chance to answer. His wife smiled at me as she put the tea in front of us. He surprised me by asking her to fix us some dinner. This time I strongly objected, and Hassanayn's wife was disturbed by my refusal. She blushed and, in a voice as soft as a gentle breeze, asked, "Why not?"

I didn't know what to say, so I gave up. Suddenly, Hassanayn turned to me and said, "Keep visiting us. I will find you a wife."

I saw his wife blush again, and felt my own ears on fire.

❈

Why did he ask me to keep visiting him? My father, his grand-father, and their whole family were saved because they trusted their fates to the will of God. Is it right that I visit him because I wish to get married? My problem will be solved by He who does not sleep, Hassanayn, and whatever God has destined will be.

Months passed, and on Labor Day I remembered al-Dakruri and almost cried. I still didn't know what al-Dakruri wanted from me, or for me. Why had he remained silent about my crimes, which could have gotten him promoted to high heaven if he had reported on them?

As usual, only the members of the workers' union attended the Labor Day celebrations. Alexandria looked grim as the summer began with sand storms that engulfed the city in sand. I prepared my fishing equipment and bought a new reel. I thought of showering Hassanayn and his gentle wife with gifts of Buri and Dinis fish. I didn't know that I wouldn't get a chance to go fishing.

Usta Zinhum walked into my office. I had almost forgotten him and, maybe for that reason, I tried to receive him very warmly, and with a big smile. Suddenly he said, "You know, of course, that al-Dakruri is dead."

I smiled, but didn't reply, so he went on: "The elections of the workers' unions are going to be held next August, and we have nominated you to be the president of the shipyard's workers' union." It took me a minute to grasp the meaning of what he'd said—president of the union. . . they nominated me!

"Me?" I asked.

"Of course," he said. I looked at him for a few moments while I scratched my head with my left hand, and then asked again, "Me?"

"Of course." Then he smiled, and I smiled in turn.

"It isn't a puzzle, Mr. Shagara," he said. "The decision has been made."

"Whose decision?"

"Mine, and that of my fellow drivers and the other workers."

I leaned back in my seat and continued to inspect him. He was very fat, almost filling my entire office with his bulk. His words come out of his small mouth as if they were pouring out of a hole in a barrel, but he talked with such self-confidence that he seemed quite comical. I became very suspicious. I remembered the day when President Sadat returned from Camp David, and how Usta Zinhum and his fellow drivers conspired against me, and how he alone, or together with the rest of them, kept the money from the workers' lunches for himself.

"What is it that you really want?" I asked him.

"Nothing. You are the best candidate for the position. Al-Dakruri didn't serve the interests of the workers. He was an opportunist who worked for his own interest."

He remained silent for a few moments after this last statement. The man was talking politics. This creep was talking politics. Al Dakruri, who had to give up smoking in order to get married, was an opportunist? Al-Dakruri, who was always pale with malnutrition, didn't serve the workers? Al-Dakruri, who allowed me and this fat hyena to steal the shipyard's money, was an opportunist who didn't serve the workers?

"Usta Zinhum, the days of the reception rallies are over," I said. "The country is in a state of turmoil, as you know. Or don't you know? Opposition, and civil strife, and every day a secret party is uncovered and dissolved—Muslims, communists, Libyan agents, Yemeni agents, and the President is insulting the people day and night. And you want me to run in the elections?"

I watched him as he put out his lower lip, then he shrugged his left shoulder. He wanted to bring his mouth close to my ear but my desk and his huge pot belly kept him at a distance.

"What's all that to us?" he whispered.

❀

The fishing equipment remained unused in a corner of the kitchen, covered with a layer of dust. Usta Zinhum had managed to wear me out. I discovered that he had more energy than I did. He always raced me into the workshops of the shipyard and called out to the workers to gather around me. They all shook hands with me with big smiles, but they never talked with me about anything. I expected them to ask a lot of questions of every kind, and to present demands, but they only smiled, shook my hand, wished me success, and then returned to their work.

I felt the absurdity of my campaign tours and thought that a kind of idiocy was taking hold of us all. Usta Zinhum said that this was normal during any election campaign.

"What is important is that the workers see you among them as much as possible," he said. This was not easy to do, but Usta Zinhum somehow convinced the engineers and department managers to allow me into the workshops and laboratories. He formed a team of drivers who printed posters, fliers, and other campaign literature that bore some of the phrases I had repeatedly seen on posters for other electoral campaigns—"Shagara is the best to represent you," and "Shagara is the workers' advocate."

Why had I gotten myself into all this? I didn't know. I just followed Usta Zinhum, who was always ahead of me. It was the first time that I'd seen all of the shipyard where I had been an employee for thirteen years—the long stretches of open space between the workshops, still pleasant despite the long tin sheets stored there, the large wooden boxes and the cranes in the air. In the workshops, I smelled the grease and oil on the floor and the workers' clothes and smelled the welding materials and the melted iron. I saw workers moving around energetically and cheerfully, bending over the huge lathing and milling machines and the cutters for metal sheets in a manner that was both friendly and humble. Many of the workers had familiar faces because they had come to my office in the past asking for some certificate or document or wanting to file one with me. I discovered the value of my own work. It wasn't just paperwork. Each of the files held a worker's life. They told of raises, promotions, and wage cuts, of sickness, absence, marriage, and childbirth. I also discovered that among the workers of the shipyard, I was the best-known administrative employee.

I spent a long time with a few workers while they assembled a ship. The sea breeze was blowing, entering our mouths and noses and going into our chests. The sea here wasn't quite the same as the sea I saw from the balcony of my apartment. Here it bustled with white ships that filled the port, their short, stocky black chimneys, and the naked chests of their sailors glistening in the sunlight. The sun looked as if it were blessing this vigorous world and the waves hitting the piers sounded like sighs or a sweet lullaby.

Every morning when I went to the shipyard I found some reason to renew my resolution to run for the elections, but at the end of every day, when I returned to my apartment with burning exhausted feet, I decided to quit. Usta Zinhum and several other drivers came to my apartment sometimes to talk about the need to buy a new piece of land on which to build new housing for the workers and the need to build a mosque in the middle of this piece of land. I only smiled and said, "*Insha' Allah.*" They also said that I should get married so that I wouldn't be lonely in my apartment. Usta Zinhum even surprised me once by saying that if I really wanted to get married, then I only had to tell him and he would take care of it all. He actually said that! I tried to ignore it. I nearly exploded and screamed at him that he shouldn't forget that he was indebted to me, and that he was seeking some personal gains out of this whole campaign, whereas I had nothing to gain from the union and the workers' problems. But I only changed the subject, telling him that I had little experience with the workers and their problems.

"Has anyone asked you any questions?" he asked.

"No," I replied.

"Then there is no problem," he said, and urged me to go to the cafés around the shipyard in such neighborhoods as Qabbari, Mafruza, and Wardiyan, where most of the workers lived. He said that this had only been done by the candidates for the People's Assembly and the local councils, that it would guarantee my victory, and that it was especially important because some of the older members of the union were making a fuss over my nomination. He said that they were spreading rumors that I was, after all, a white-collar employee who knew little about the workers, that I was not one of them even if I didn't have a college degree.

This sounded like a serious matter, but I had a feeling that Usta Zinhum was lying. Nobody seemed very concerned about these upcoming elections, neither the union members nor the workers, the engineers or the managers. Everyone just shook my hand with a wide smile and wished me success. No one really discussed anything important or asked me why I was running. The only thing that left a significant impact on me was that I had spent more than a hundred and fifty pounds on publicity so far. I did what Zinhum wanted me to do, but I wasn't going to retreat. Now I wanted to be the president of the workers' union. My first decision as president would be that the shipyard never take part in reception rallies again. I would put an end to Usta Zinhum's dreams.

I began hanging out at cafés until midnight, when I would return to my apartment completely exhausted. All I found at the cafés were workers who were there to play backgammon or dominoes, cheer for the winner and boo at the loser. They always invited me to have tea or coffee, and I always insisted on paying for all the drinks. One of them turned to me once and said, "The most important thing, Mr. Shagara, is that you do something for Imbabi."

"Who is Imbabi?" I asked.

"Don't you know him?"

"No."

He looked at his colleagues in disbelief and then said, "He is the oldest worker in this shipyard. His is quite a story. Poor Imbabi!"

I remained silent, so he went on: "Fifteen years ago, when this shipyard was still a new project, the land was still part of the sea, which they were filling. Trucks came loaded with stones and dirt and dumped them into the sea. Imbabi was one of the workers who leveled the newly filled lands. He had just moved from the south with his younger brother. One day, his brother fell into the water and could not be rescued.

The divers never found him, and the sea never threw the body back to the shore in any part of Alexandria. Since that day, Imbabi has never left the shore. He comes in before any of the other workers to sit in front of the water and call out: "Imbabi, Imbabi." His brother too was named Imbabi. He slaps his cheeks and his eyes remain fixed on the water and the fishing lines he sets to catch fish. He sets several lines and ties the end of each line to a large rock so that the fish can't run with the line. Every time one of the lines moves, he quickly pulls the fish out of the water, crushes it with a piece of stone, then throws it back, as far as he can, into the sea. At three o'clock exactly, Imbabi pulls his lines out of the water and prepares to leave with the other workers, his face red and his hands cut and scratched. He still doesn't believe that his brother is dead, or that the fish that ate him will never bring him back. But how come you didn't know about Imbabi?"

The story, in fact, came as a complete surprise to me, and for a few moments, I thought that the worker was lying, but another worker said, "What do you want him to do for Imbabi? The shipyard still pays him his salary even though everyone knows that he hasn't worked in fifteen years. Do you want him taken to the mad house? The man is old and has lost his teeth and most of his eyesight. He will die sooner or later."

❋

That night, I heard a movement in the apartment next to mine. The next morning was Friday and I woke up early even though I had become accustomed to sleeping later since I decided to run for the elections. I stood on the balcony with the idea of watching the sea, but I saw four pretty young women hanging their wash out on their balconies and exchanging greetings. So the building had filled with neighbors who had come to know each other. What a terrible thing I was doing to myself—I, who came home in the middle of the night dragging my feet like two sacks of sand, woke up early, when the men who had these beautiful wives were still asleep! I thought that exhaustion was of two types: one makes you go to sleep just to get rid of it, like a machine that is turned off to rest for a while, which is what I did, and another that puts you to sleep and takes you to the land of sweet dreams, and that type was for the husbands of these women.

※

The date of the elections drew near. All I cared about then was that they would be over so that I could get some rest. I had already spent two hundred pounds on publicity. I had no way out of it now. I consciously avoided going near the sea in my tours. I didn't want to see that Imbabi. In fact, I sometimes became very enthusiastic about the campaign despite the indifference that prevailed around me. I was overcome by a strong desire to win for a reason which I cannot reveal now. I didn't notice that my visits to the different cafés often took me near Hassanayn's house in Qabbari. Once, when I was sitting at the Lansh Café with a bunch of workers, all smoking *ma'asil*, their mouths opening strangely to blow out the smoke as they talked, I saw Hassanayn walking toward me with his pleasant smile, "You are here, so close to my house, and haven't come to visit me?" he asked. I held his hand and invited him to sit down. A moment later he noticed the workers gathered around me and was a little confused.

"Hassanayn, a friend of mine," I said, introducing him.

"We know him," a few of them said. "It is only he who doesn't know us." They started telling him where each one of them lived while he became even more confused and started to blush. I was annoyed by this useless talk.

"A campaign effort," I said, and he only smiled. I knew that he didn't believe me, or rather didn't understand what I meant, but the workers started talking to him about their pride at being represented by me, telling him about the conspiracies against me and their efforts to sabotage these conspiracies and defend my reputation. "Mr. Shagara isn't distant from the workers. He knows them better than anyone. He has the files, and the files have everything about everyone." This was the first time I heard about any conspiracies against me. Hassanayn led me out of the café, and said: "Why didn't you come over? Ibtihal chose two girls for you to meet, and we had it all arranged."

"I came more than once, and couldn't find you, neither at home nor at the café. I told Magid about it and asked him what you were doing."

"Magid never told me a thing," he said, and after a pause I asked, "What should we do now?"

"Nothing," he answered. "Both girls got married. It's summertime, and the expatriates returning from the oil countries snatch up everything that isn't nailed down!"

That made me laugh, after my anxiety. It struck me that he was trying hard to help me, but I couldn't be too upset with myself. As he was preparing to leave, he turned to me and said, "By the way, Hagg Luqman used to sit at this café in his early days. I will come visit you some day."

※

I heard loud knocks on my door. I wondered who could it be at six o'clock on a Friday morning. For a moment I felt scared. I had no parents, siblings, or relatives who could be at the door. Annoyed, I went to open the door.

"Garbage?" said the man who was standing there in an incredibly dirty *galabiyya,* with an old jacket over it and carrying a large basket. I was confused for a moment, then I said, "There isn't any."

Then I closed the door and stood in the middle of the hallway. So a garbage collector is now coming to our building. It has filled with residents who have made such arrangements for daily life, and I didn't know. Until the day before, I had been throwing my garbage into the sea. I needed sleep badly. The night before had been election night, and I had won with the highest number of votes. I went back to bed, and fell asleep immediately.

10

Two beggars sit near the public urinals in Dikhayla. One of them was once a well-known grade-school principal who used to open the school at night and force the teachers to lecture to the empty seats. The other was a butcher who heard a sheep cry between his hands as he was slaughtering it. He said that it was a ram sent by God from heaven. A few days ago, the two men became four.

"How can you sleep when you are the president of the union?" Hassanayn cried as soon as I opened my door. I put out my hand to shake his, but I didn't embrace him. He had not embraced me when I went to his house to congratulate him on his marriage.

"A terrible summer flu," I said. He held my arm and I leaned on him until I managed to return to the bedroom and lie down in bed. I pulled the covers over me, then asked him, "How did you know?"

"By chance. One of the people I had met with you at the Lansh Café stopped me on the street, shook hands with me, kissed my cheeks, and then told me. He was very happy. Are you taking any medicine?"

"I don't like medicine. I just drink a lot of lemon juice."

We were silent for a few moments during which Hassanayn looked at the old furniture around the room. Why hadn't I bought some new furniture? I had savings I wasn't using. Hassanayn stood up, and his smile became wider, so I smiled back at him and said, "Don't you dare suggest that we go to the café."

"I won't," he said, "but let's at least go out on the balcony. This room is very grim, and it must be infested with germs. I have a sensitive chest, as you know. Besides, you won't get better unless you expose yourself to sun and fresh air."

He pulled the comforter off of me and pushed it into a bundle at my feet. Then he tried to pull me by the arm.

"All right! All right!" I said, laughing, but with difficulty, my whole body shaking. "I'll get up." I supported myself on my hand and sat up on the side of the bed. Hassanayn tried to pull me again, so I was forced to get up. I was about to lean on his arm when he moved it away.

"Walk on your own. I will carry two chairs," he said. "You're not as sick as you think."

I walked to the balcony on my own, wondering about Hassanayn and his strange behavior.

"It was the mistake of my life, Hassanayn," I said as soon as we had seated ourselves on the balcony. "It really was. I can't find time to work or sleep. They come to me here with their problems."

"Listen," Hassanayn said, "I didn't come here to listen to

you complain. I came to tell you that we have several potential brides for you, so if you're serious we should do something about it, and if not, then let's just go to the café and forget all about it."

I watched him as he talked. I was happy to see him. He seemed to be more concerned about me than I was about myself.

"Many things have changed for me since I got married," he said. "The most important of them is that I don't think alone anymore. My mind no longer goes on asking and answering questions until it's exhausted. Now I think out loud. I talk to Ibtihal and then I feel better. Thinking is now a sweet exchange. You know what? I have noticed that women usually smile when they're talking. Before my marriage, I had never noticed this. Your wife's smile makes you relax and appreciate the beauty around you. At night, when we're in the same room, the light seems to be very bright. It becomes white, whiter than milk, and I feel the contentment of someone who has everything. I nearly forget that there are other people, other rooms, a whole world full of sadness and joy around me. Our room becomes an island in a sea of bright light.

"I'm not trying to tempt you into marriage," he went on. "You seem to be quite ignorant about life, but we have come to the point after which it is all downhill. Now we have to run to catch the train of normal people. It is a wonderful train, and on it you find real life, no matter how late. The real tragedy is if you miss it. Do you realize what it means for you to become forty years old without a son? It means, at the very least, that you will not live long enough to see him become a man. I don't think that anyone in our generation will live to be more than fifty. The number of changes in the presidential cabinet that we have seen in our lifetime alone is enough to shorten the life of an elephant!"

His last statement made me laugh, even though laughing made me ache. I was following what he said, amazed, and wondering what went through his mind to make him talk to me like this, as if I were opposed to the idea of getting married. But he went on: "Don't laugh. I'm serious. Where do you think they get all these ministers? They must out-number normal citizens. Anyway, this will all be to our advantage on the Day of Judgment. God will stand in front of all the people and ask each person what his or her nationality is. Egyptians will be allowed to enter heaven with-out judgment because of what they have suffered on earth, especially with the change of cabinets. Don't laugh! In addition to our inevitable suffering, we also make things more complicated for ourselves, because we actually have it better than others. Each of us has a stable source of income. Magid has his pharmacy and can find an apartment if he wants to. 'Abd al-Salam will return, and you'll see that the first thing he'll do will be to get married. We have an advantage over many people, and even they get married. They may complain about their inability to do so, but before long they invite you to their wedding. Then they go on living however they can, but never give up. They are a race of jinni children who can pass through the eye of a needle.

"Besides, what's keeping you from getting married?" he asked. My whole body was already rocking with laughter, and I was desperately trying to signal him with my hand to stop. "Don't let the union make you believe that you are a great activist. That may happen. Weren't you arrested for political activism? You must know that this isn't your kind of thing.

Holy Yahya is more suited for it than you are, and 'Abdu al-Fakahani is the best of all. Even if you want to be an activist you need to get married. Napoleon was married, and so was Lenin, Sa'ad Zaghlul, and even the prophet Muhammad, who set a record. And why should I go so far? President Nassir was married and had children. Huh! President of the workers' union! Who cares? Hagg Luqman has become a member of the People's Assembly. God damn you, bastard!"

I was completely overcome by both laughter and coughing. Hassanayn looked as if he had just taken a weight off his shoulders, and he sat back with a satisfied smile on his face. I remembered the five hundred pounds, but only went on looking at the sea in front of us. The waves were smooth and the sea seemed to be asleep and dreaming. There was a refreshing breeze in the air. September was holding on to the last summer breezes, while cautiously opening the door for fall. I felt that sitting here might cure me of the damned flu. I felt that I was not sitting with Hassanayn alone, but with Magid and 'Abd al-Salam as well. Oh, how we all loved each other without even knowing it.

"Can you believe that it has been almost a year since I last saw Magid?" I asked. "We are only five minutes away from each other, but for some reason I don't go to see him, and he doesn't come to see me either."

"I saw him at the pharmacy before I came to see you," he said as he stood up. "I was upset with him because he had not told you about the two girls, but he said that he had come to see you twice, but you were out. He also said that every day he thought of passing by to see you, but then hesitated, thinking that maybe you would come by his pharmacy, until he forgot about the whole thing."

"Hassanayn, please," I implored. "I can't laugh anymore."

"Then don't laugh," he said.

"O.K. O.K. Have you ever known me to be a liar?"

"The biggest liar in Egypt and the whole Arab world as well."

"O.K., but now I want you to believe me. I only want two things: the first is to get married and the second is to quit the union."

I went to visit Hassanayn, and he wanted me to choose one of two women: the first was a beautiful young widow, who wore a veil and had an apartment, a child, and a large bank account left to her by her former husband, who had drowned in the Tigris. The second was a typist who was not as pretty as the first. The widow was twenty-four, while the unmarried woman was twenty-six. Hassanayn innocently told me that ever since I had told them the story about the man who threw his furniture into the sea, he had been thinking of finding me a wife, and that he had been serious when he mentioned it the first time. He also whispered to me that if Ibtihal hadn't been his cousin, he would have preferred me to himself and let me marry her, because he saw me as a child who is lost in the desert. He was not serious about what he said, but I still felt embarrassed. First he had thought that I didn't want to get married, then he thought that I was incapable of finding a wife. He had done all but take my hand and wander down the streets calling out: "A woman for this miserable man!" This paternal attitude of Hassanayn's annoyed me, but I still said that I wanted to see the unmarried woman. Hassanayn laughed when I told him my choice and said in a voice that was loud enough for his wife to hear: "The widow's husband drowned in the Tigris. Is this our fault? And why did he have to swim in the Tigris in the first place? Couldn't he have swum in the Euphrates?" I heard his wife laugh in the next room. I hadn't thought that the unmarried woman was better than the widow; it was more like a random choice. Perhaps if I had thought about it carefully, I would have realized that the widow was better. She was prettier, richer, and already had a child who would therefore be easier to raise. Who knows? I thought that maybe I would be like my father, unable to have a child for twenty years. We made an appointment for me to see the woman the following week.

※

The day on which I had planned to quit the union drew near. I had been thinking about quitting since the very first day after I had won the elections, but couldn't reveal my thoughts. To be honest with you, there were times when I changed my mind, but for the most part, I could not stand what I had to handle: absences, sicknesses, social aid, dismissal warnings, requests for leaves, organizing recreational trips to Port Said, suggestions for literacy classes and other classes to help the workers' children with their school work. Where had all these responsibilities been and how come no one had mentioned them to me before the elections?

I spent my days running between the various workshops and administrative offices of the shipyard. I finally realized why al-Dakruri had been so thin and pale, and thought that his death was inevitable. If the snake hadn't bitten him, he would still have died soon from a heart attack. My office was always full of workers who came in to tell me about their problems, but also took the opportunity to chat and enjoy a few laughs. I didn't have time to take care of the employees' files, which became covered with cobwebs and made my office look like a haunted house.

My apartment filled with workers who thought that a private meeting with me could help them get a promotion. Usta Zinhum always brought so many of them that I sometimes wondered if he were not just bringing people off the streets. My time and energy were completely wasted on these new responsibilities. I wasn't used to this mess. I was used to silent papers placed in neat files that I could open at any time. I arranged them and changed things in them and they never objected.

At the end of one long day, as I was getting ready to leave the office, Usta Zinhum came running in. He was sweating and out of breath. I suddenly wished I had a bed in my office so that I would never even have to leave!

"A crisis, Shagara," he said. "A real crisis."

I felt my whole body tingling. He had just called me by my name without bothering to use Mr. or any other title.

"What happened, Usta Zinhum?" I asked.

"Imbabi is dead."

"Imbabi who?"

"Imbabi. Don't you know him?" He pulled up a seat and sat down, then said to me, "Have a seat first."

I had already remembered Imbabi, about whom one of the workers had told me during my campaign, when Usta Zinhum said, "Imbabi, the lunatic. He was found dead on the beach, his body surrounded with crushed fish, his mouth reeking with the smell of fish and covered with clotted blood. Now dozens of workers are gathered around the body. They say that he had recently started to eat the fish raw, and that today he ate so much that it bloated him. The problem is that nobody knows his address or any of his relatives."

I pointed at the files and asked him to look under "I" and "M," then sat back in my seat and let my arms relax to my sides. The round man bounced like a rubber ball and soon he pulled out a file, placed it in front of me, and opened it.

"The file only has one page," he said. I looked at the sheet of paper, which only had his name, age, job, and salary at the time when he was first hired. There was no address, and there was nothing to indicate any change in his life: a marriage, a promotion, sickness, punishment, transfer. Nothing. There was only one yellowed sheet of paper, partially eaten by weevils.

"This is what I expected. The union will take care of his burial," Usta Zinhum said while I watched him silently. I wanted to slap him on the face, he who knew everything, that spy!

Burying the man wasn't a difficult job. I left Usta Zinhum to handle it and went home. I looked in the mirror and couldn't ignore the paleness of my face, which reminded me of al-Dakruri's. I had no time to cook and lived on canned foods, although I often read in the papers that they weren't well preserved and not fit for human consumption. The other members of the union didn't help. They only passed the workers' problems and demands on to me. I had to wait for the chairman of the board of shipyard directors to fulfill his promise to consider "the files" its own department and staff it with two more employees. I would be the head of that department and the supervisor of those new employees. The shipyard had placed an advertisement for these two new positions in the newspapers, and it was going to be a few more days before the promise could be fulfilled. I was waiting for that to happen before I quit the union. Then the chairman wouldn't be able to go back on his decision. Actually, he could, but I didn't think that he was going to. God was still on my side. I thought that I could sue the shipyard if the chairman went back on his decision, because I would have the right to keep my new position. Yes, I would defend my rights, because a person who doesn't defend his rights is worthless.

The important thing was that my marriage plans developed quickly. I visited Hassanayn at the time that we had set, and found Nawal there visiting with his wife. Before I had had time to think about how I could introduce myself, Hassanayn called to his wife, "Why don't you both come and sit with us?" She smiled, left the room for a minute, and then came back with a china plate that I had seen before, bananas piled upon it. Nawal followed her into the room and shook my hand.

Would anyone believe that that was the first time I had shaken hands with a woman? I was thirty-five years old, and had shaken the hands of many of my female colleagues and many of my mother's female neighbors in the hills, but none of them had made me feel like a man shaking hands with a woman. Nawal's hand was warm and it trembled a little. My hand was as cold as ice. I looked at her face while she looked down at the floor. She was as small as a cat, and sat with her knees and her legs pressed tightly together. She was pretty, and her eyelashes never stopped fluttering. She must have sensed that I was watching her. She must have been aware of my ulterior motive. Who knows? Maybe she was also looking at me somehow. I wondered whether that year, 1980, was going to be a decisive year in my life.

It seemed as though I was always trying to remember some-thing, but couldn't. At work, at home, with Hassanayn, when I was alone with Nawal at her house, I often had the sudden feeling that there was something I wanted to remember, but I didn't know what it was.

"We came to celebrate," said Hassanayn as he opened his arms wide and embraced me. It had been a while since we had embraced. I had heard the doorbell ring repeatedly and thought that it was Usta Zinhum coming to me with a new problem. I decided that I would beat him up, and if I could, throw him and his buddy off the balcony. But when I opened the door I found that it was Hassanayn and Magid. Magid and I embraced several times, and then I went in to get two of the old chairs, which were going to be replaced in a few days, but Magid said, "Let's go to the café. The café is better." I realized that I could see a few white hairs among his shiny black hair. I stood in the middle of the hallway without getting the chairs. It was as if Magid had paralyzed me with what he just said. What was the secret of that little, mostly empty café overlooking an ordinary road where cars raced by? I had a lot to talk about with both of them—how Nawal and I were going to buy a refrigerator, how we were going to buy a stove, how we had bought china and kitchenware and chosen some nice simple furniture that we were going to buy in a few days in cash, for I was going to withdraw all of my savings out of the bank. My account was back at a thousand pounds, after having decreased during the election campaign. Nawal's father and her brothers were going to contribute another thousand pounds. I also wanted to tell them that I hadn't had time to go by to see Magid and invite him to the wedding, which was coming soon, but that I would have definitely remembered to do so before the wedding date. We hadn't had an engagement party, but had only exchanged rings in the presence of Nawal's close family. The wedding, though, was going to be attended by members of both families, and mine was Magid, Hassanayn, and 'Abd al-Salam.

This is too much for a chat in the café, Magid, I thought, so why do you want us to leave? I have found Nawal to be quiet and tender. I want to tell you how I kissed her for the first time, and how she was surprised and confused, and how I have tamed her so that she now puts her head on my chest and nestles like a bird, and how my arms can almost cover her up. Here we are, going to the café to chat about the same old things.

"Is it really December already?" I asked, and Hassanayn smiled at my question and said, "You are already starting to see the days differently."

"It is hard to believe that this is December in Alexandria," said Magid. "It rained constantly last December, and January too. Alexandria has gone crazy." Then he laughed and added: "So, you're finally getting married, Shagara."

He rolled the dice and threw them on the backgammon board. Once again, I had the feeling that I was trying to remember something but couldn't. I lit a cigarette and smiled as I rolled the dice in my hand.

"What's up?" Magid asked, having noticed my absent-mindedness.

"I was thinking that I wish my mother were still alive," I said. Then I threw down the dice and went on playing. I didn't know what had made me say that, but Hassanayn patted my shoulder, and blushed. Then he said to Magid, perhaps to change the subject, "Have you seen the house of jasmine lately? It was pulled down, and now there is a vacant lot in its place."

I was suddenly depressed. I hadn't realized how long it had been since I last walked down that street. My feet just got used to their new route. I tried to concentrate on the dice as Magid played.

"We saw it on our way here," Hassanayn said to me. "I'm sure you know the house."

So he knows the story of the house, I thought. Magid knows it, too, and so does the rest of Alexandria, just as 'Abd al-Salam said.

"If Magid got married, and 'Abd al-Salam returned and got married as well," I said, trying to get the conversation on to a lighter subject, "then we could all have children who would grow up together."

"Allah! Allah!" cried Hassanayn, "You are as good as Hassan al-Imam." We all laughed as loudly as we used to, but it was not long before we were silent again. Then Magid said, "Not a single word from the American woman."

His statement surprised me and Hassanayn. We had forgotten about the American woman and her promise to Magid. I looked down at the dice on the board and could feel that Hassanayn was looking at me.

"Dr. Musa has written to me a few times from Kuwait, trying to tempt me to join him there," Magid went on, "I'm seriously considering going."

It became impossible for me and Hassanayn to go on ignoring what Magid was saying. He was holding the dice in his hand and waiting for our comments. I wanted to say something, but felt that if I opened my mouth, I would scream.

I looked at Hassanayn, who was blushing and looked unhappy. Hassanayn took a letter out of his pocket and said that it was from 'Abd al-Salam.

※

"War has broken out between Iraq and Iran, as you probably know. You must have read about it in the papers or heard about it on the radio and television news. I can't believe that you're so busy that you haven't had time to write to me for so long. My only explanation is that you have separated. If so, then I wish each one of you all the best with his new life. Who knows? Maybe you really don't have time.

"Anyway, I'm sure you know that I have a lot of experience with war by now. It seems to be my destiny. God created me, and said: 'You, 'Abd al-Salam, are going to be a warrior,' and so He gives me an opponent everywhere, even when I don't really know it. So far, I'm still not sure exactly who my enemy is. What is certain is that I'm a brave warrior, and this is enough for me to fight any war. I'm the bravest warrior in the Middle East, and if there is no war, then I will have to start one. I must be the bravest warrior in the world. I have volunteered to fight in the Iraqi army.

"Don't be surprised. I know that people travel to make money, and then return home, but I'm not like them. I'm different. I'm a warrior first and foremost, and so war follows me wherever I go. Must the best years of my life be spoiled? This is my destiny, and I cannot fight it and become like everybody else.

"I know very well that if I'm taken prisoner, the Iranians will kill me as a mercenary, and that if I get killed, the Iraqis will consider me to be a martyr and glorify me. I know that, and I'm comfortable with it. What bothers me is that I don't know what you will say about me. What will my own people say about me? If you asked me, I would tell you that I don't like death and I don't care for glory. The problem is that you are so far from me, and that I still don't really understand what the word 'homeland' means exactly, so please forgive me."

I went home at the end of the evening thinking of what 'Abd al-Salam wanted from us or what he was doing to us. I felt a sudden nostalgia for a walk on the street of the house of jasmine to take a look at it, even after it had been demolished, but I couldn't do it. 'Abd al-Salam's letter had left me quite sad. What exactly does "homeland" mean?

I wanted to write to him. I had a particular thought which I wanted to share with him: If you die, 'Abd al-Salam, I will never have any rest. I'm bound to you with an umbilical cord. People do travel far, but only to make some money, return, get married, and settle down. You almost said that yourself, 'Abd al-Salam. Then they have a homeland, even if it's small. Yes, marriage is the homeland, and people make their own homelands. I will be married in a few weeks, and will have a homeland. Oh, 'Abd al-Salam, what a liar I am! Now you have made me wonder how many years of life have passed while I was in exile. Where was homeland before? Marriage by itself cannot make a homeland at all. . . I will not write to you, my friend.

It was almost midnight, and it was starting to rain.

Epilogue

I stood on the balcony looking at the sea, which had awakened as early as I had and invited me to look at it. The sea is always relaxed and relaxing. It doesn't share anyone's anger or joy. There was only a single lonely ship in the distance and it appeared to be the master of the universe.

I will teach my son to swim in you in his first year. From the very beginning, I will let him face the waves, for we only have bad times ahead. My son, read this book of mine to learn all about your father, and don't blame me. My story was never the story of a marriage, or else it would have been a big farce. Search for the secrets hidden between the lines. My marriage to your beautiful mother was the easiest thing I have ever done... Don't forget that my father, your grandfather, planted my seed but it took twenty years to sprout. But you were different. You put an end to my fear and announced your arrival on the first day. It was as if you had been hidden in some secret corner of the universe waiting to jump out in the dark, as if you had been sitting at the feet of God, and no sooner did I plant your seed than you jumped out, almost exploding from your mother's belly. Remember that you are different from me, even if you are my offspring, and don't be like me. . . I am certain that you are a good son. And don't blame me. This house is from another house which I had sold by force, so it may be haram. This is furniture bought with money made by force as well. Read so that you will learn, and don't blame me. The most certain thing is that you are all halal. And don't ask how your father managed to preserve his sanity and not go crazy.

I jumped up in the air and ran in to the kitchen where Nawal was, with her big round belly, fixing a delicious breakfast.

"Breathe in this air," I told her as I put my hands, which I had cupped as if I were carrying water in them, to her nose. She looked at me in surprise, then laughed and stepped back.

"Breathe in this air quickly," I said again, and this time I was also laughing. I saw her molasses eyes gleam with surprise.

"You're nuts," she said.

"You don't understand. Come on, quick."

"Shagara, have you lost your mind, sweetheart!"

"Breathe. Then I'll explain." I brought my hands closer to her nose, and she couldn't retreat any further because of the kitchen wall behind her. Her belly prevented me from bringing my body too close to hers, but my hands were right in front of her face.

"Deeply," I said, and she took a deep breath. I felt the air flowing out of my hands, turning them cold as ice. The teapot was boiling on the stove, its cover rattling with the steam.

"I talked to my son on the balcony," I said. Her eyes became wider.

"Then I gathered my words from the air into my hands, and wanted to send them to him. Was there any other way of doing it?" Nawal kept on laughing gaily.

"You are really nuts," she said. "And how do you know it's a boy?"

"I know it is," I replied. "I will call him 'Ali, tell him to name his son Muhammad, and he will tell Muhammad in turn to name his son Shagara. This way, there will be another Shagara Muhammad 'Ali in the third generation. Shagara will then have a son named 'Ali, 'Ali will have another Muhammad, and Muhammad will have yet another Shagara, and so the names of my grandfather, my father, and myself will be repeated once in every three generations."

Nawal was watching me in great surprise.

"And why all this?" she asked. I kissed her on the cheeks, and grabbed my fishing equipment.

"What about breakfast?" she cried.

"I am happy today, and don't need any breakfast."

※

I went down and saw the expansive space, its arms wide open. All that white mixed with soft blue, I thought. All this sweet air that tempts me to jump up and swim in it. What a fool and a loser I am! I suddenly realized what it was that I had been trying to remember for so long. It was the hundred pounds that I had hidden in a mattress five years ago. That was what I had been trying to remember, what had been distracting me all along. The hundred pounds were now lost forever. I had sold all my old furniture to a secondhand-goods vendor who rarely comes near the sea, and even if I met him, he would probably already have sold the furniture to another vendor. I stopped.

And what if I had found the money? I bought an apartment without it, got married without it, and will have a son without it as well.

Twenty years ago, one of our neighbors lost a hundred pounds, so his wife set herself on fire. It was the price of a plot of land that he had inherited. At that time, many people were killing themselves with D.D.T. The husband ran like mad, grabbed a blanket and wrapped it tightly around his wife. The poor man had not realized that their one-year-old baby was wrapped in that blanket, and that he was standing on top of the baby after it had fallen out of the blanket between him and his wife. He didn't understand why his wife was screaming hysterically as she tried to push him away and grab her baby. He did save his wife, but she lived wishing that she had died, and he always seemed lost and unfocused after that... God! These times were long ago. No one would try to kill herself for a hundred pounds today. Besides, it was my fault that I lost it, and I shouldn't let it spoil such a beautiful day. I walked on, and almost bumped into Holy Yahya coming from the old street on which I never walked anymore.

"Hey, it's you," I said. "Are you still alive?"

"People like us don't die Mr. Shagara. I was coming to see you."

I stopped to look at him carefully. His clothes were all new and clean.

"Welcome. Let me walk home with you," I said, trying to be nice.

"That won't be necessary," he said. "I wanted to congratulate you on your marriage, and I also wanted to tell you that if you have any friends who want to buy apartments, I would be happy to help them. You are a good man who deserves only the best, and I would be happy to have tenants like you."

I was still looking at him. He was talking to me as if we were friends just because I was trying to be nice to him. The strange thing was that he seemed sincere, and really had been coming to visit me. I almost laughed as I remembered Hassanayn saying that Holy Yahya would make a good president of the workers' union. I tried to imagine him with his tiny figure up to his ears in the workers' problems. My resignation from the union had come as a surprise to a lot of people and they had tried to convince me to change my mind. Usta Zinhum tried especially hard, but I told him never to try to contact me again for any reason. I was right when I guessed what the chairman of the board would do. He didn't go back on his decision to make the files into a whole department, and I now enjoy new privileges as head of that department.

"Are you building a new apartment building now?" I asked Holy Yahya.

"Yes. On this street, in place of the house of jasmine. You must have heard of it. I bought it and will build an apartment building in its place."

I took a few steps backward. There he had spoiled the day for me.

"I bought it for myself this time," he went on. He was smiling in great confidence and pleasure.

"I will try to find some tenants among my friends for you," I said, trying to get rid of him. Hundreds of tons of stone, iron, and concrete were going to be placed on the most beautiful face I had ever seen. I wondered where that woman with the beautiful face was now. Was it really true that I could have married her? But there wasn't any woman in the world more beautiful than Nawal. Was there?

I walked on. I sighed deeply as soon as I had walked away from him and thought of returning home without fishing. What did it mean when a scoundrel like that owned a house older than you or me, as 'Abd al-Salam had said? But I kept on walking.

Nothing should spoil my pleasure with the pure happy breeze around me, or with the wide-open space. Let the house of jasmine be owned by all the thieves in the world. There will never be a person as depressed as the owner of that old house.

Translator's Afterword

The publication of this translation of *The House of Jasmine* in 2012, not long after the January 25th Revolution that resulted in the ousting of President Mubarak on February 11, 2011, is an opportune and fortunate event. *The House of Jasmine*, first published in 1984, chronicles the beginning of many of the social and political practices that the 2011 revolutionaries hope to bring to an end.

The House of Jasmine opens in Alexandria on June 13, 1974, the day American President Nixon visited the city, accompanied by his host, Egyptian President Sadat. Nixon had flown to Cairo the day before and with his secretary of state, Henry Kissinger, met with Sadat and other top Egyptian officials. On the following day, the *New York Times* carried news of the visit: "Arriving in Alexandria yesterday, President Nixon received a rousing welcome from hundreds of thousands as he had yesterday in Cairo." The *Times* reporters, perhaps in an attempt to improve the tarnished image of the "Watergate president," called the visit "triumphant" and interpreted the Egyptian reception as an indication of the people's trust in Nixon, the harbinger of future peace and prosperity in the region, and of Sadat's popularity with the Egyptian masses. The novella tells a different story: a story of deception and fraudulence, planned by a scheming administration and carried out by a disenchanted and dejected population. The novella's protagonist, Shagara Muhammad 'Ali, is but one representative of that population.

Shagara's father died in 1967, shortly after the June 5th defeat that marked the end of an era of Nassirist optimism. In the same year, Shagara quit school, began working in the new shipyard, and had to move with his mother to the hills of Dikhayla, where they lived in a poorly constructed house that neither of them liked. When Nixon arrives in Alexandria, seven summers later, President Sadat has succeeded President Nassir, who died in 1970. Egypt has fought another war with Israel, a war that began with an Egyptian military victory and ended with an American-brokered cease-fire, and Shagara is a low-level administrator living a life of utter indifference. He has no ambitions or hopes of his own, and no friends except for the similarly disillusioned trio, Hassanayn, Magid, and 'Abd al-Salam.

Abdel Meguid's novella is an indictment of the Sadat era (1970–1981), an era of rampant corruption, when only salesmen and those who have no scruples about making a quick buck can advance, while people who uphold any principles or ideals, Shagara and his friends among them, are bewildered and alienated. Hassanayn seeks refuge in books of history and later in marriage, while both Magid and 'Abd al-Salam seek a way out through emigration. Shagara becomes a small-time crook in a land of major-league criminals. Ironically, his redemption comes during the course of what went down in official Egyptian history as an "uprising of thieves."

On January 18, 1977, massive demonstrations erupted in both Cairo and Alexandria. The demonstrations were protesting the increase in the price of bread and other basic food products, including sugar, flour, and cooking oil, that had been announced by Sadat's government the day before. Upon the advice of the IMF and the World Bank, the price hike was meant to reduce the budget deficit through a reduction of the government subsidies on these products. It was in these demonstrations that Shagara, the aimless loner, finds himself part of a larger and purposeful group:

> "Oh!" I say, trying to hide my smile and my inability to understand. I find myself forced to advance toward Sayyid Birsho and the flood of angry workers pouring down Maks Street. Traffic is blocked, and passengers stream out of the tram and stopped cars. The windows of the houses overlooking the street are thrown open, and faces of women and children appear in them. They're repeating the slogans, and I too am chanting along with Sayyid Birsho.

Shagara gets arrested for his participation in these demonstrations, but he is not convicted, most likely because of the testimony of the shipyard's chairman of the board of directors, who claims that Shagara only participates in the official rallies that show public support for the president. Shagara's participation in the demonstrations makes him realize that what legally vindicates him, morally incriminates him:

> I had almost shouted out that I was really the one who incited all the demonstrators, that I was the one who pulled up the lamp posts, tore out the sidewalk tiles, burned transportation vehicles, night clubs, and police departments. I don't lead official rallies, as he said, but only cheat, and I've never even gone to any of them.

Shagara refuses to participate in the rallies that were organized for the reception of President Sadat upon his return from Jerusalem in November of the same year. His refusal is, at least partially, inspired by his realization that there is something honorable in the demonstrations opposing President Sadat's government and something dishonorable in orchestrating rallies in support of it.

The House of Jasmine serves as a counter-narrative to the official history of the Sadat era. Besides telling a different story about Nixon's reception, it also portrays what Sadat and his state-sponsored media dismissed as an "uprising of thieves" and the minister of the interior claimed was the result of "attempts by hostile forces to spread rumors and incite the masses," as instead a genuinely popular revolt by the Egyptian working class to defend its basic everyday needs. The January price hikes, which the government announced and then was forced to rescind because of the popular uprisings, were only part of a larger economic policy aimed at liberalizing the Egyptian economy. This policy had its beginnings in 1974, when Egypt received its largest loan from the IMF on the promise that it would privatize Egyptian industries and institutions that had been government-owned and -run under Nassir's government, to reduce government subsidies and other services, and to give private investment a free rein in directing the Egyptian economy. The result of these liberalization policies was a rapid concentration of wealth in the hands of the few and an increasing income gap. Egypt became a country of net imports and its main export became Egyptian labor, both skilled and unskilled. There is no indication in *The House of Jasmine* that Shagara understood any of this when he took to the streets with the workers from the shipyard. He probably didn't. He only had a gut reaction, an intuition that compelled him to be one with the protesting masses.

As part of its function as counter-history, the novel also provides an alternative narrative of how Egyptians received the news of Sadat's visit to Jerusalem in 1977, and the Camp David agreement of 1979, two moves whose popularity with the Egyptians were "proven" to the West through support rallies not different from those that received President Nixon a few years earlier. In its function as counter-history, *The House of Jasmine* is not alone. Much of modern Arabic fiction contains more truth than the region's official state histories, which have been produced during regimes that have traditionally enjoyed almost full control of the media. Particularly notable Egyptian novels that challenge the country's official historical narratives include Sonallah Ibrahim's *The Committee* and *Zaat*, Radwa Ashour's *Specters*, Ibrahim Abdel Meguid's *The Other Place*, Idris Ali's *Dongola* and *Poor*, Khairy Shalaby's *The Lodging House*, and Alaa al-Aswany's bestseller *The Yacoubian Building*, among others. Each of these novels, like *The House of Jasmine*, represents in its own way an era of corruption, political repression, and a systematic state effort to disseminate misinformation and falsify history.

The Sadat era was the precursor of Mubarak's rule, for, unlike Sadat, who reversed the general direction of his predecessor's policies, Mubarak followed in the footsteps of Sadat and continued many of his policies and practices throughout his thirty years of government. Readers of this English translation will be reminded of the rallies of "Mubarak supporters" that poured into the streets of Cairo after his maudlin speech on February 1, 2011, supposedly without promise of compensation, to counter Tahrir Square revolutionaries who continued to insist that Mubarak step down. They will be bemused at the way the state-sponsored media in 2011 attributed the anti-Mubarak protests to "hostile forces" and foreign provocateurs, almost exactly reproducing Sadat's official discourse on the 1977 bread riots.

Readers will also find that Shagara's account of his participation in the 1977 demonstrations could have been excerpted from any number of the accounts of the millions of Egyptians who participated in the 2011 demonstrations. It tells of the same feeling of unity that the protestors experienced in 2011. It recounts the violence initiated by the Central Police, and even includes many of the same slogans, chanted in 1977 and again more than thirty years later, calling for freedom, social justice, and a government that does not forge or falsify the attitudes and aspirations of the people.

Stendhal once wrote that "politics in the middle of things of the imagination is like a pistol shot in the middle of a concert," yet Abdel Meguid's novella empties its gunload of politics into the narrative without disrupting its harmony or detracting from its merit as a work of literature. This is largely due to Shagara's narrative voice. Shagara has a good sense of humor, and the reader easily identifies with his shyness, sadness, and frustration, and with his modest wishes for a place to call home with a wife and child. His narration is often funny and never encumbered by political ideology or discussion, perhaps because he simply does not have any, but is only trying to make sense of a world that is rapidly changing and growing uglier by the day. He searches for simple beauties, a female face, a memory of a childhood romance, the scent of jasmine, and other small and fleeting pleasures. He is also disarmingly honest and often acts and speaks on impulse rather than after any serious deliberation.

The reader can partake of Shagara's bewilderment at a world he barely understands through the vignettes presented at the beginning of every chapter. These vignettes are independent of the main narrative and of each other, but are not unrelated. We may wonder whether the naked blond woman who comes back to life after being hauled out of the canal in a sack, and who then is futilely chased by the locals, represents President Nixon's promises of prosperity. Or whether the drunken dogs who proved faithful to their dead owner and his anti-imperial slogan are a contrast to President Sadat's government, which reversed Nassir's socialist and non-alliance policies only a few years after his death. We may wonder long and hard and not arrive at a definitive interpretation. Yet while we wonder, we will also be laughing. In our puzzlement and laughter, we will be very close to our protagonist, Shagara Muhammad 'Ali.

Acknowledgments

I wish to thank Mark Pettigrew and Jim Saliba for their helpful suggestions and edits to this translation. I am also deeply grateful to Hilary Plum at Interlink Publishing. Working with Hilary has been a pleasure and has certainly made this novel a better read. Thank you.

Noha Radwan